Daughter

of the

Revolution

By
Becca Patterson

Daughter
of the
Revolution

Copyright © 2013 Becca Patterson

Cover design by Annette Kavanaugh

First Print Edition September 2014

Acknowledgements

I would like to extend my thanks to Ekaterina Beauomont, Devin Harnois, Sarah Bella, Lori Dahm-Milligan and Elizabeth Sogard for their help in getting this story out of my head and into your hands. I would also like to thank all the people who make NaNoWriMo wonderful every year.

CHAPTER ONE

TRISTAN - ROYAL TRANSPORT

"Your highness, could you please pay attention?" Master Keiren called Tristan back to the report on Graylan County.

"Sorry." Tristan put down his tablet and looked up at his governance master. "You were telling me about Lord Phillip Leblanc. He has been governor of the county Graylan for the past forty years since his mother died unexpectedly. He has one daughter, who will be graduating in the coming year, with his wife, Lady Richia, who is second heir to County Threvail. They are also my closest living relatives, which means I really should have seen more of them growing up." Tristan smiled at Master Keiren's expression. "County Graylan specializes in rare metals. They have numerous asteroid belts that attract mining operations. The Others have several outposts within County Graylan, but there have been no known incidents of trouble between Humans and Others."

Tristan picked up his tablet again.

"So you were paying attention." She sighed. "You should make more of a show of that."

Tristan shrugged. "Why? If everyone thinks I'm a goof, it'll give me more room to play."

"You are the next monarch. Play isn't your focus."

"Says you." Tristan let the tablet drop to his lap. "It's playing if I know what everyone else is planning and they don't even think I care. Politics is a game. Besides, I've been studying the counts since I was three. What I need to know, and you can't tell me, is how to make Uncle Phillip like me so he won't oppose me as king." Tristan took up his tablet again. The report he really wanted to read was the latest from the Graylan research team who had noticed a change in Others' behavior toward human traffic.

"Sire, you need a better attitude."

"About what?" The tablet landed back on the table with a slight thud.

"About your duties. About your life."

Tristan glared at the woman. "How about the fact that unlike everyone else my age, I'm not worried about what major to choose. Or about the fact that I won't sit down with a school counselor to see what career I will be best at or happiest doing? No, those things were decided the day I was born. No aptitude or attitude test required."

Master Keiren stood up to glare back at him. "You should feel lucky that you don't have to face that stress."

"I don't."

"Do you know how many...?"

"...Teenagers out there would love to be in my place?" This would get back to his mother, but he didn't care. "They only think they do. They don't want to make the hard decisions, but how many of the navigation majors out there would really like to be in governance? Or music majors, or research, or communications even?" Tristan turned away from Master Keiren. "We're done."

"Sire..."

"We're done."

Master Keiren bowed herself out the door. Tristan knew she would use the extra time to compose her message to his parents. It wouldn't go anywhere until they shifted back into normal space and then there would be the delay of interstellar communication and politics. The response would come sometime after his meeting with Lord Phillip Leblanc of County Graylan.

Tristan flopped to the floor to feel the gentle hum of the ship. How much fun it would be to discover something like Middle Space where a whole new set of physical law governed. Or to be the one to crack the language barrier between humans and Others. He would love to just be there when they found something new.

The door opened, then closed again. *They don't even know me well enough to look down.* He went back to daydreaming about what he could have been.

A knee on his chest and a hand around his throat brought him back to reality.

"You've dismissed Master Keiren early again." His chief of security sat on him. "And you aren't practicing self-defense

2

either."

"Get off." Tristan pushed against the small man to no effect. "Master Allay isn't scheduled until after dinner."

"A terrorist is going to get herself on your calendar before attacking?"

Tristan scowled. He tried pushing again, still with no success. Then with a sigh, he shifted his hips and shoulders and sent Mr. Kenchi rolling. Tristan rolled himself into a ready stance. "I said get off."

Techani Kenchi, the newest member of Tristan's staff, sat back against the wall and laughed. "That's better."

Tristan didn't fall for it. The man could launch an attack in his sleep. "Why're you here?"

"Your masters think I'm the only one you listen to."

"You're the only one who listens to me... sort of."

He laughed again. "You're upset?"

Tristan backed up against the opposite wall and slid down to sit on the floor. "I just want to be normal."

Techani nodded but said nothing.

"I want to take the aptitude test, find out what I'm really good at—what my career should be based on *me,* not my parents. I want to go to class in a real high school, study for tests, not meetings, and maybe just once fail at something. I just want to go to the mall."

"I can help with that last one."

"What?"

Techani smiled. "You want to go to the mall like a normal kid. I get that. Maybe buy some clothes for yourself or at least a pair of shoes that hasn't been focus tested."

Tristan nodded.

"There's only one problem. You are the prince and the most recognized face in the galaxy."

Tristan dropped his head onto his knees. "So I can't go to the mall."

"No, that means you can't go to high school. The mall is easier, especially since you made such a fuss over that toddler you brought with you."

Darryl was the son of his favorite attendant. Mal, a single father, was transferred out of Tristan's entourage because he didn't have appropriate care. Tristan fought back and forced the palace planners to make a space for the boy on the transport. Since then, Tristan had fallen for the boy and spent as much time as he could scrape together playing with him.

"I made a fuss over keeping Mal, not Darryl."

Techani shrugged. "All the same to the gossip columns." He rose to his feet as though gravity didn't affect him. "Now that he's here, we should make official use of that fact. And we'll make it look like you planned it right from the start."

"I don't get it." Tristan clambered to his feet too.

Techani activated the display on the tabletop and started drawing a map. "Prince Tristan can't go to the mall—too many political gas pockets."

Tristan nodded, half afraid they weren't going to the mall.

"But Trevor Calloway and his little brother can."

"Who's Trevor?"

The display changed and two images of boys popped up. One the official image of Tristan that was flashed all over everywhere, the other a boy who looked a lot like him.

"Trevor is you—without the formal clothes and with hair that hasn't been touched by a stylist for at least a week."

"My stylist won't allow that."

Techani reached across and mussed Tristan's hair. "Mr. Green will kill me for that."

Tristan looked for the nearest reflective surface to see what had happened. His hair was a mess. It was great! He went back to see what Techani was planning.

"This will work best right after your meeting with Lord Leblanc and before the state dinner."

This trip was going to be stellar.

#

TRISTAN - MALL

Tristan all but jumped out of the car when it pulled up to the massive building. The building itself was bigger than the palace, and there were so many doors and people coming in and out. It was the chaos that kept him from running off on his own. He'd never done anything like this before. Out with the people and only one security guard anywhere he could see.

"Trevor, help with your brother." Techani stepped out of the car on the other side. He was completely comfortable in the casual shirt and slacks he wore. Bright colors that would never be seen together in the palace, even on staff.

Tristan's outfit was a little more subdued. A black button-up over an electric-blue undershirt that showed where he didn't button the top buttons and a pair of jeans. He was still wearing his black leather shoes because they couldn't find anything else that fit him. Techani had even managed to convince his parents to release a budget for him so he would be able to buy better shoes today. Darryl was in his usual cute shirt—this one had a teddy bear on the front—and little jeans anchored with red running shoes.

Tristan released the straps on the safety seat and pulled Darryl out of the car into a big hug.

"Big," Darryl said, pointing to the mall.

"Yeah, it's big." Tristan laughed. He stared at the building the same as Darryl. It was bigger than the palace, but there were no security features. The palace was surrounded by open space and a wall where the guards checked everyone entering and exiting. Here people just walked through the doors, sometimes bumping into each other.

"You two really are a pair." Techani brought over the stroller. "Stop staring or you'll call attention."

Tristan dropped his eyes and concentrated on getting Darryl into the stroller. Darryl concentrated on making that as difficult as possible.

"Big." The boy pointed again.

"Yes, it's big."

"Big." This time he was pointing away from the mall.

Tristan looked where he was pointing. The royal transport hung over the city like a little palace of his own. No wall but secure all the same since it was separated from the shuttle port by almost a mile of empty air. From here it looked imposing.

Then it was gone.

The first force of the blast pushed Tristan into the outer wall of the mall. Moments later the thunder of the explosion hit him again. Where the transport had been, there was a cloud of red and gray. Tristan pulled himself up, swooping Darryl into a great hug. He watched in horror as the burning shell of his ship fell from that cloud, setting off another roll of thunder and lifting a second cloud into the air.

Techani grabbed him by the shoulders and dragged him into the mall. Inside, people were running toward the doors. Techani pushed through the crowd to the first clothing store. He tugged Tristan to the back and pushed him into a dressing room.

"What happened?" Tristan asked.

"You just got lucky." Techani looked over the little door. "Stay here, and quiet him down."

Tristan hadn't noticed that Darryl was screaming. "Shush,

it'll be all right." Except Tristan didn't believe it. He concentrated on keeping his breathing calm. "Hush now, you aren't hurt."

Darryl stopped screaming, shoved his thumb in his mouth, and laid his head on Tristan's shoulder. Tristan rubbed his back and wished that someone could hold him like that.

"Here, put these on." Techani threw some clothes over the little door. "They won't fit, but don't complain. We have to hurry."

"What? Why?" Tristan started changing as he asked.

"Someone just tried to kill you."

Tristan didn't want to think about that. He pulled the too-small, gaudy printed T-shirt over his head and the too-big pants up his legs. The outfit looked atrocious and would be hard to walk in if the pants started to fall down.

"What do we do now?" he asked when he came out of the dressing room.

"We go anywhere people won't expect you."

#

EMALYNN - SCHOOL CAFETERIA

Emalynn set her tray on the table. The gelatin jiggled a bit, but the soup stayed in its bowl. She loved when the cafeteria had tomato soup with grilled cheese sandwiches. She didn't love when the soup sloshed all over the tray and pre-soaked the sandwich or got all over the salad. She looked back toward the serving line to be sure Karen and Dom had seen where she'd gone before settling into her seat. Dom was fussing over the salad bar as usual. She could be so picky it was a wonder she ever ate. Karen waited patiently for Dom to choose a bite of broccoli. They made such a cute couple, but Emalynn didn't know where Karen found the patience to stay with Dom.

Emalynn waved. Karen waved back.

By the time Dom and Karen found their seats, Emalynn had already finished her salad and was working on their Public Communications homework.

"You're not revising your persuasion project again, are you?" Dom asked.

"No." Emalynn lied. She didn't mention that she'd already spent more than half an hour today adjusting the images.

Karen laughed. "You know our Ly." She put her arms around Emalynn's shoulders with a little shake. "She just has to be perfect in everything she does."

"I don't want to risk my graduation." Emalynn put her

tablet on the table next to her tray. She recognized the mistake two seconds after Dom snatched it up.

"So what are you working? Oh…" The look on Dom's face made it hard to tell if that was a good "oh" or a bad one.

"Give that back." Emalynn reached for the tablet, knowing full well that Dom would pull it away. She counted on it. The tablet went into safe mode automatically.

"Hey," Dom complained when she saw that the screen was dark. "How'd you do that? Is that one of the ninja tricks your Baba teaches you?"

Emalynn laughed and took the tablet out of Dom's hand. "It's not a ninja trick and Baba's not a ninja. It's a tech trick that Murphy showed me."

"Oooh, borrowing your boyfriend's tricks now? Next thing you know you two will be making wedding plans." Karen made a kissy face. "I'm going to be in the wedding, right? I mean, we are best friends and all."

Emalynn ignored the comment while she set her password again and shifted the tablet over to her navigations homework before setting it back on the table, away from Dom.

"I think you offended her," Dom whispered to Karen loud enough for the kids in the washroom to hear.

"I'm not offended, I just don't have anything to say."

"Right. Why are you always so worried about your grades anyway?" Karen asked.

"Because I know what happens if you don't graduate."

"Yeah, we all know. No graduation means no citizenship." Karen threw up her hands. "It's not like they kill you or anything."

"They might as well." She tried not to think of it, but tests always got her worried.

"What are you so negative about?" Dom nudged her.

"You don't want to be *ungraduated*. It's awful."

"Right." Dom rolled her eyes. Emalynn could get really annoyed with that girl. "You saw all those poor non-citizens when you and Baba were traveling the universe."

"Exactly," Emalynn said. She didn't tell them Baba was ungraduated or what she did for a living. It scared her enough without having her friends as possible witnesses.

"So you hired non-citizens for some housework or what?"

"Not exactly."

"Tell us."

"I really don't want to talk about it." She dug into her sandwich, dipping it a little too far into the soup.

"Then why did you bring it up?"

"I didn't." She let the soup drip for a moment. "Did you see the news?"

"You mean about Prince Tristan?" Karen was always up on the latest to-dos. "It's just awful. The death toll is up in the thousands and they're still searching."

"Did they find him yet?"

Karen shook her head. "There are lots that haven't been ID'd yet. It's been days. You'd think if he were alive, they'd say something. I mean, he's the only heir."

Emalynn shook her head. "So? Someone else will become heir. They have lists for that, don't they?"

"You don't get it. Other monarchies had to keep detailed lists of the potential heirs. But we've evolved past that. This will be the first time in the history of the monarchy that they've had to look beyond the immediate family. And it would have been the first time since the beginning that we had a king to king transfer. It would have been so historic."

"You're just saying that because you think Prince Tristan is cute," Dom teased.

"Was cute," Karen said.

They all fell silent again. Emalynn considered turning her tablet back on.

"Have you had your counseling appointments yet?" Karen asked.

"Not yet," Dom said. "I'm scheduled for tomorrow."

"Mine was this morning," Emalynn said. "Why?"

"I have to go this afternoon." Karen looked about as thrilled as if she'd said she was going to the dentist. "I'm not ready to decide the rest of my life yet."

"It's not that dire." Emalynn assured her.

"That's easy for you to say."

"No, really. All they do is look at your grades and help you see what you're good at. That's what they use to help you figure out your major."

"So what's your major?" Dom asked. "Communications? No wait, you spend too much time revising for that to be it."

Emalynn rolled her eyes. "It was only the first appointment. My grades show that I could do communications, but I'm really more cut out for physics or any science other than biology."

"Wait, you aren't good at biology?" Dom covered her open mouth with her fingertips. "That's got to be a first."

"I got an A in biology. I just didn't like it."

"Science." Karen stuck out her tongue. "Ugh. Why would you even want to do that?"

"Because I'm good at it. I actually like the sciences. And Navigations is fun. I'm submitting my course for the midterm today and I think I've got a good chance to take the top spot in class."

"You are a weirdo." Dom pointed at her with a fork full of pasta.

"You would know. So are you," Emalynn shot back. "Have you ever managed to go a whole day without plotting out a new vid?"

"Hey, I've got important things to say."

"So you'll be a communications major."

Dom suddenly found the ceiling very entertaining.

"Um, yeah, that's going to be a problem." Karen kept her voice low. "Her parents think that communications is a second-class major. They've been fighting a lot."

"Oh. I didn't know," Emalynn said. "But don't let that deter you. Just because your parents don't agree, that's no reason not to do what you love. It's your life."

"Yeah, it's my life, and if they don't like it, they could sell me to some corporation, just like an orphan."

That killed Emalynn's appetite. The others stopped eating too. She couldn't help thinking of Charlie, who'd been "adopted" out to a corporation at the start of the term. He didn't even get a chance to clean out his locker. Emalynn hoped he'd get lucky and graduate anyway, but she doubted it. Even if he did, he'd probably be in so much debt he'd never be able to leave the company.

"See you in communications," Emalynn said as she gathered her plates. She slid her tablet into its pocket and headed for the washroom window.

"No more editing," Dom called after her. "Have fun in Navigations."

"You have fun in physical arts."

"Wait." Karen hurried to catch up. "Seriously, what do you think I should major in?"

Emalynn stopped to look her friend in the eyes. "I don't know, but you do enjoy the arts classes. Think about that."

"But I'll need a good apprenticeship." Karen dumped her tray in the window with a little too much force. "Your life depends on your apprenticeship."

"You'll find one, when you decide what you want. Your life depends more on your goals than anything else." Emalynn quoted Baba's advice.

"Do you think it will hurt?" They moved toward the door.

"What?"

"The injection."

"I imagine it's just like getting all the regular shots. Just a bit more important."

"But it's a virus. Viruses can kill."

"No one has ever died from the graduation marker." Emalynn looked at her friend. She hated the system that punished anyone who didn't pass that last test with non-person status.

"Don't look at me like that." Karen snapped her out of her thoughts.

"Like what?"

"Like I've made the worst mistake of my life for questioning graduation."

"Sorry, it wasn't you. I was questioning the whole system."

"You really should take the governance major."

"Ewww. I don't think I could handle that."

"But you're always thinking about the greater good. You have such good ideas and you're a natural leader. And looking like Prince Tristan could only help."

"I do not look like Prince Tristan."

"You should look in a mirror more often." Karen waved as they split to get to classes.

#

MURPHY - SCHOOL LOUNGE

After school, Murphy found a spot in the student lounge and spread himself over several comfy chairs. He only needed to be a chair hog until Emalynn got there, and most people knew the pose. There were others striking a similar pose on other sets of furniture. He could recognize most of them as friends of the cheer squad, MultiBall team, and debate club—the three major activities that had second shift today. They were all waiting for their friends to come for the in-between study session, just like him. By tradition, the teams and their friends got the lounge, so anyone waiting for a first-shift team got to hang out in the library.

Dom kicked his foot when she arrived. Time to sit up and

actually pull up his homework. He had a biology test tomorrow and he hoped Emalynn and Karen would help him study. They'd passed biology last year with their friend Charlie—poor Charlie—helping them out. He hoped they remembered enough to get him through the genetics unit at least.

"What's up for today?"

"Biology."

"See ya." She started to leave.

"Hey." Murphy waved her back. "Just because you passed it last semester doesn't mean you can't help out a little."

She smiled and came back. "I may have passed it, but I know you have to be on genetics and that part totally confused me." She plopped into the seat across from him. "I mean, that whole part about identical twins. I still don't get it."

"What's to get?" Emalynn asked from behind Murphy. How long had she been there? "Identical twins have exactly the same genes. That's all."

Emalynn floated around the chair and sat next to Murphy, snuggling up to him to look over his shoulder at the tablet.

"Yeah, well, if they are identical, why are they usually male/female?" Murphy asked.

"'Cuz that's not genetics. That's hormones. You'll get to that next." Emalynn tapped on the screen to bring up the article about gender. "See here."

Murphy read. He should have been long past this and into his major classes, but he'd hacked himself younger so now he was stuck taking biology. He read the article twice just to be sure.

"So it says there used to be a gene that coded for gender. Then it failed. How can a gene fail?"

"It gets mashed about by mutations until there aren't any good copies left. You really should remember your history better. You remember the start of the monarchy?" Emalynn pulled the tablet all the way out of his hands and started pulling up several articles.

"See, this you should remember from history. The male crash. It lasted several hundred years and humans almost died out because males were so sickly. The gene for male gender carried too many faulty genes and males, even when they were born, only had a fifty percent chance of making it to adulthood. Got that part?" She pushed that article with a cool icon to one side.

"Right. So men were weak, sickly doobs who needed to be coddled."

"Something like that." She cuffed him on the shoulder. "Then one family started having a lot of strong healthy males. Naturally, they became powerful. And when their sons had more healthy sons, they became even more powerful. At the time, it made sense to follow them because they must be doing something right."

Murphy didn't quite agree with that logic. Then he saw the sparkle in Emalynn's eye and realized she was tweaking him. "Right."

"So that family became the head of government. Go down a few generations and humans were starting to spread over the galaxy, and they decided we needed a central government to keep it all organized. Well, who do you think they chose to lead that government?"

"The guys with strong guys."

She laughed. It always made his knees melt when she laughed.

"Wait, so just 'cuz they had men who could walk on their own, they were seen as better leaders?" Dom squeezed in on Murphy's other side.

"Basically, but that's not genetics; it's history. Here's the genetics part of it. That family had a new mutation in the gene that coded for female. That gene could go either way—male or female. All the diseases and weaknesses associated with the male gene went away. The men were just as healthy as the women."

"Great, but people can't just switch back and forth. So how does it decide?" Murphy asked. He could feel the frustration tightening his shoulders.

"Hormones." Emalynn passed the tablet back to him.

"How does that work?" Murphy felt like he was about to explode.

"Well, men and women give off different pheromones, and they trigger different hormones in a pregnant woman." This time it was Karen who snatched the tablet and pulled up the relevant vid. "So if she's around more men, she has the hormones that trigger the female part of the gene, and if she's around more women, she triggers the male part. Only, when she has twins, they affect each other most of the time. One will choose female and the other becomes male in response. That's why most twins are male/female. You can only tell the identical ones because they look so much alike."

"You mean like Emalynn and Tristan?" Dom asked. She didn't sound so innocent, and the way she ducked even before

Emalynn could swipe at her proved she was baiting Emalynn.

"I do not look like Tristan." She complained. "Besides, my birthday is two weeks after his."

"Teasing." Dom stuck out her tongue.

Actually, she looked almost exactly like him. It was one reason Murphy had become her friend, to see if she fit the rest of the profile.

"True." Karen stopped more than an arm's length away. "You have better hair."

"Oh really?" Emalynn crossed her arms and pouted.

The others just fell apart in laughter.

"Don't you wish that it could be true, though?" Murphy asked. "I mean if the prince had a long-lost twin sister..."

"It'd be all over the vids, even now. You think the royals would really let something like that happen?"

Murphy wanted to tell her how it happened. But he couldn't be sure. Not until he met Baba. Emalynn promised she'd introduce him to her tomorrow.

"No." He admitted.

"So do you get your genetics now?" she asked.

"Not really." He lied. "I'm still working out the alphabet."

She smiled in that way that told him she knew he was lying. He pulled up the articles they were supposed to test on tomorrow. She leaned in close and started going over them with her. Karen and Dom took the hint and cuddled on the other chairs until it was time for them to head down to the gym.

CHAPTER TWO

EMALYNN - HOME

Emalynn drifted along the hallway, still high from practice and the thought that Baba would be home tonight. She might already be there, cooking one of her rice meals. They were nothing to post about, but they were simple, cheap, and delicious. More than that, they were love. She had bought fresh tomatoes yesterday just in case.

The halls of their building were quiet as always. The other residents worked all different shifts, so they slid in and out of the building quietly. She'd only seen about half the people who lived on their floor, and only when they gathered for holidays. Yet something made her slow her approach to her door. He stomach tensed as she reached out to have her ID read. She dropped into a ready stance as the door slid open.

Blood on everything, still warm enough to smell. Their few treasures in pieces on the floor. What wasn't smashed was tossed about. Baba had fought with everything she had. But there was nothing left. The door slid closed, letting her forget, for a moment, the full horror.

I have to leave. She backed away from the door. *They might be waiting. I have to leave.*

She ran down the hall—no plan, no idea other than to get away. When she emerged at the base of the stairs, she composed herself. All of life is an act for the camera. Today she was playing the excited teenager off to see her boyfriend. It wasn't much of a cover, but it might slow them down just enough for her to keep ahead. That was as far as she managed to plan—get to Murphy before the authorities realized she was an orphan.

#

Emalynn woke warm and comfortable. The alarm hadn't gone off yet, so she lay in bed, enjoying a slow wake-up. Something tickled at the back of her mind, something she should remember. She opened her eyes into the shadowy darkness. They were shadows that didn't belong in her room.

She bolted upright, ready to pummel anything that moved. The lights came up on the sports idols of Murphy's room. It all came flooding back. The smell of blood just before she opened the door. The sight of it spattered all over the apartment. The blood alone would have been proof of murder. She squeezed her eyes shut, trying not to remember the pieces. The scene was still there, in all its gory detail. When she opened them, the tears flooded out. Her throat closed around her grief as she curled in on herself.

Warm arms held her while her body shook. They rocked her when the sobs quieted. Murphy wiped the tears off her cheeks and held her close. When the worst of it was over, she pulled herself together and wiped at her stray tears. They left muddy streaks down her arms. The dirt she'd used to make a quick color change to make it harder to trace her through the cameras was ground into Murphy's sheets.

"I'm sorry," she whispered, trying to brush it away.

"For what?" He pulled her back into a hug.

"I made a mess. I'm a mess. Oh dear." She looked down to see that she'd covered everything with mud.

"Don't worry, we have a shower you can use."

"But I don't have any clothes."

He held up a stack of folded cloth. "Aunt Maggie's about your size."

"You told her I was here? I told you not to. She's going to have to report me now."

"She noticed your footprints."

Emalynn bit back the rest of her rant. She didn't have a plan or money to make it happen.

"You should probably take your shower. Your shuttle leaves in just over two hours." He planted a light kiss on her forehead. "I'll explain my plan over breakfast."

"Your plan?" She had her doubts.

He smiled and pushed a towel into her arms.

The water mixed with dirt and created a runny ooze

that looked a little too much like blood. She closed her eyes and let the water run down the drain unseen. She scrubbed until it hurt, then just a little more to be sure. The cool draft when she stepped out helped to steady her nerves. Maggie's clothes did fit well, though they weren't a style she would have chosen. All the better for remaining unnoticed.

She brushed out her hair and started to put it up. *Down will hide my face better.* She brushed it back down so it covered her face. Then she made her entrance to the dining room.

Maggie swept her into a hug. "Murphy told me about the trouble with Baba. I'm so sorry."

Murphy emerged from the kitchen carrying two plates of pancakes with sausage. He gave her a look that should have meant something. She didn't have a clue what he was trying to say. She glared back at him to tell him he was still on her bad side. He smiled back, looking a bit relieved.

"I do hope that when you get to her, everything will turn out fine. Don't worry about paying us back for the tickets. It's the least we can do for you," Maggie continued. "Well, I'll be off, then. I'm a bit behind in the office and even a few minutes late will cost me. I've called you both in to the school office so everything should be fine." Then she was out the door.

Emalynn stared after her. "What did you tell her?"

"That there was an accident and Baba is in the hospital on the transfer station in Defari." Murphy looked too pleased with himself over that one. He set one of the plates of pancakes in front of her and the other directly across. "Did you want juice?"

"Of course." Her stomach reminded her that she'd only had an energy bar last night. "Your plan?"

Murphy made a show of pouring the juice and making sure everything was set before he sat down too. Emalynn was already halfway through her pancakes before he started.

"Your plan." She prompted again after clearing her mouth.

"I have some friends who travel a lot. Tabby is a freelance journalist and Claire is her camera operator. They just happened to be in the area. I didn't tell them anything more than that you needed a quick apprenticeship."

"I'm just supposed to trust them?"

He swallowed hard before answering. "No, but do you have any better plans?" The look of confusion meant he hadn't thought it through.

"I mean, do they even know what they're getting into? I don't know who's after me and you're going to put your friends

17

in danger like that?" She stabbed at the sausage. "How am I supposed to know who they are? I don't know who's after me or what they look like."

"I didn't..." Murphy gestured with a bite of pancake.

"I'm sorry." Emalynn set her fork down and pushed away from the table. "I didn't mean to snap like that."

"It's fine. I was stupid." Murphy didn't look at her. "But it will give you some legitimacy. An internship, they can't arrest you for that."

She didn't like it, but she couldn't argue it either. "I can't stay with them for long. And I'm not a journalist."

Murphy smiled. "They know. They don't really want a real apprentice anyway. You'll just carry their bags and they'll pretty much ignore you until you come up with something better."

She still wasn't so sure about this. "How am I supposed to know them?"

"I'll send you pictures. It won't be that bad."

"You can't send anything to my tablet. That's traceable."

"But you are going to be legit."

"The authorities aren't the only ones chasing me."

"Oh." He poked at his pancakes.

Emalynn sipped her juice.

"Take my tablet."

She raised her eyebrows.

"No, listen. They'll trace it and find me. I'll be conspicuous so the cops find me first. Then I'll just say that we were being cute and I don't know where you are."

She shook her head. "Then they'll trace your tablet and find me."

"But it'll take time. Besides, you can wipe it once you're on the shuttle to the transfer station. By the time they figure that out, they'll have to start fighting for jurisdiction."

Emalynn was impressed and more than a little creeped out that he knew that much about the system. The question was out of her mouth before she'd even decided she wanted to know.

"There's a reason I'm living with my aunt." He smiled.

#

MURPHY - SHUTTLE PORT

Murphy sighed with relief when Emalynn waved from the other side of the security gate. She would like it on Galica, and his parents would make sure she graduated safely. And she would make a great addition to the Alecti Army too.

He tore himself away from the shuttle port. He had to make his alibis for last night and this morning. But first, he needed to ditch her tablet. Not just ditch it, but destroy it. He pulled it out at the train station and "tripped" near the rails so the tablet fell onto the track. The next train roared into the station while a small crowd cringed about his poor lost tablet.

"That's gonna hurt." A woman patted him on his back.

"Major loss," another commented.

Murphy waited until that train left to be sure the tablet was in enough pieces. He caught the next one back into the city.

"You dropped it onto the train tracks?" the clerk at the tablet store asked again to pass the time while the computers did their work tracing Murphy's ID to his financial account.

"It was so stupid." Murphy enjoyed telling the story. "I was just trying to get away from the crowd so I could hear the vid better and I tripped. I shouldn't have been doing my homework on the train anyway."

"That is pretty sad." She pouted for him.

"Worst part is, it's my girlfriend's tablet. We switched to be cute for a day, and now I'm going to be so dead."

"You're going to owe her more than just a replacement."

"Well, this is an upgrade." He pointed to the tablet he was waiting to take possession of. "And I'll be leaving her a few nice little surprises when I reconfigure it."

"You taking the programming major?" The sales clerk's eyes lit up.

"I'm considering it. I still have a couple weeks to decide."

"I always think guy programmers are cute."

"Thanks." Murphy smiled.

He took the tablet as soon as he could and left. Would she have been so flirty if she knew who he really was? Probably, but it would have been different. He started the reload for his security protocols and private programs. The process was only halfway done when he got home, so he turned the apartment console to his favorite news channel.

"And in other news, an unidentified woman was murdered in her apartment in the Roshea neighborhood."

Murphy pinged on that. Emalynn had lived in Roshea.

"Neighbors are shocked by the violence that attacked this quiet family. Police are asking for anyone with any information about this murder or the location of her daughter to contact them immediately."

The picture changed from the shot of Emalynn's apartment entrance to an ID shot of the woman.

He knew that face. He'd been forced to memorize it and all the projections for how it might age before he even left his home on this mission to find the princess. That was the mercenary they'd been looking for. If she was the one murdered like Emalynn said…

"Oh hells."

One idiot who couldn't follow local traffic laws had missed the scheduled meeting. They'd been looking for her ever since. A skilled mercenary changed her ID often, so tracing that was out of the question. They'd been looking for her face in news reports and crowd shots ever since.

"It was a brutal killing, leaving the entire apartment covered in blood and gore." The picture shifted to a shot of a cleanup crew entering an apartment building. "The woman who held many aliases, including Adelle Topondreas, Caval Jurgan, and Baba Algrian, also had a daughter. She has not been seen since last night. Authorities are now seeking information on the whereabouts of this daughter, Emalynn Algrian."

"Oh no. No. No. No!"

Murphy grabbed the tablet off the couch. He didn't have enough credits left. The house terminal was keyed to Maggie's account. He'd have to make up for this later. This was exactly what they were all looking for. She'd forgive him for buying the ticket to get the princess back.

The next shuttle didn't leave for another six hours. He bought a ticket anyway and kicked the couch out of frustration.

He went to his room, grabbed a bag, and threw some clothes in it. He hoped that would be enough. He should call Tabby and let her know.

"Come on, come on, answer already." The tablet went to message.

"Tabby, change of plans. Wait for me. I'll be there as soon as I can. Special circumstances."

"Where are you going in such a rush?" Maggie asked when he nearly knocked her over on the way out.

"I've got to catch up with Ly." Murphy tried to push past her, but she muscled him back into the apartment.

"No, you don't." She took the bag from his hand. "You have a mission to do here. She'll be fine."

"You don't understand. She is the mission."

"Three days ago, you were ready to move on. She's not here, you said. What changed?"

Murphy growled in frustration. He turned the terminal back to the news report he'd been watching. He waited just long enough for the dawn of realization to hit Maggie before he grabbed his bag and slipped out of the apartment.

CHAPTER THREE

EMALYNN – TRANSPORT SHUTTLE

Emalynn had made good use of the six-hour shuttle flight. Six hours without a net connection gave her more than enough time to completely wipe the memory on the tablet Murphy gave her. She reset it with the security protocols Baba had taught her. It would have been faster if she'd had access to her net drives, but that was why Baba had taught her to do this from memory.

When the shuttle clamps locked down and the net came back, she looked for the pics Murphy promised he'd send. They weren't there. She was the last one off the shuttle, still waiting for the pics to show up. She would just have to slip past everyone and find another way to hook up with Murphy's friends. Or maybe it was time to cut that life entirely. Move on to the next one.

Always know who is around you. Especially when you are moving from one life to the next. Baba's voice cautioned from the back of her mind. It was a lesson that had served her well all the times they'd traded one life for another. Learn the politics fast and land the biggest bully on her back as soon as possible to keep the rest at bay. That last part wouldn't help now, as any fighting would bring unwanted attention, but knowing who was who…

Most of the passengers ahead of her were tourists, aside from the occasional business traveler. The others coming from other shuttles were the same. No one looked liked a film crew or what she guessed friends of Murphy would look like. Two women caught her eye. They were dressed as business travelers but had a focused air about them—like hidden security before a raid. Emalynn tried to hide behind a large woman until she could get past them.

"There she is." The words rang out over the din of

conversation.

One of the women was pointing straight at her. Emalynn ran down the corridor against traffic. She ducked through the crowd until she found a service corridor that led to the loading dock. She slid behind a stack of crates to catch her breath. The crates were stacked in front of a bank of lockers. She tried the doors until she found one that opened. It was filled with overalls in a variety of sizes. She picked one that was a little big and pulled it on over her clothes.

She stepped out into the corridor and continued down the curve. She'd gone past five or six bays when she heard people up ahead. She turned back where she came from, hoping the costume change would be enough.

"There you are." The women she'd been running from met her just around the curve.

Emalynn attacked. She caught the first woman with a fist to the chest. She spun to backhand the second in the face. She ducked and swept her leg around to knock the woman to the floor where a last palm to the side of the head put her out. The first woman was just picking herself off the wall when Emalynn slammed her back into it. She fell to the floor in a heap. Emalynn checked for a pulse in each of them to be sure they were alive. A murder charge would be unforgivable.

She heard more voices from the passenger end of the corridor. *Not good, not good at all.* She'd have to take her chances farther down the cargo bays.

She rounded the corner right into a large woman holding her tablet like a shield.

"I'll dock your pay if you don't get back to work right now."

"Yes'm." Emalynn played along. She joined the line of workers hauling crates from the corridor through an airlock. She kept her senses open, searching for any sign that she'd been found.

"What's all this?" the crew supervisor yelled as Emalynn made her fourth round.

"Have you seen this woman?" A security guard showed the supervisor a tablet.

Emalynn kept her head down and brought the next stack of crates in. She slipped away from the other workers and hid among the crates. She was able to shift one stack so there was a hollow in the middle just big enough for her to squeeze inside. She just had to hide long enough for security to check all the legit workers and move on.

"Where are we going?" Tristan asked as they approached the first security gate. Techani had woken him early this morning, saying only that they needed to get to the shuttle port.

"On a cruise."

"You're kidding, right?" Tristan stifled a yawn.

"No. What better way to keep you moving and the rest of the galaxy guessing?" Techani smiled the way a villain does when explaining his master plan in a kid's vid.

Tristan shook his head. He'd wanted adventure, the chance to live a normal life. Now he was getting the adventure, but all he really wanted was his security team and home. Traveling as a normal citizen was full of firsts. His first time passing through the normal security gates, using his ID chit, being scanned as though *he* might be a terrorist.

They dropped their bags in the scanners and stepped through, sliding their left hands under the scanner—just like in the vids.

They passed into the travlers' section of the station. The stream of passengers spread out. There were little stores lining the halls, just like at the mall.

"Why do we need to keep moving? Can't we just go home now?"

Techani stopped to look at an outfit displayed in a window. "We don't know who your enemies are. That makes home the most dangerous place for you."

Tristan felt his stomach twist at that thought. "But we didn't know my enemies before either. And there will be more guards there."

"It's getting there that could get you killed." Techani continued down the corridor. "Until we know who we're dealing with, we can't know who to trust. Any of the guards at the gate could be your enemy. Or any of the communication techs."

Tristan felt the world drop out from beneath his feet. It was almost worse than when he'd seen the explosion. He'd been killed. Only he was still here too.

They came to the second security gate. The line backed up into the corridor.

"They're going to ask your relationship to Darryl." Techani warned. "Call him your cousin."

"I thought he was my son."

25

"There was something at the last gate." Techani looked around. "Cousins are easier to believe if they check his background."

Tristan nodded. So they were cousins now. Tristan said that to himself several times. The line moved forward slowly. Tristan caught a glimpse of the guards at the head of the line. Three of them were talking to each passenger as they approached.

"Am I supposed to know where we're going?" Tristan asked.

"Tell them it's a surprise for your birthday."

"But my birthday is months off."

Techani just smiled.

Tristan couldn't be sure if Techani was joking or serious. He didn't ask anything more as they moved forward until it was their turn. Techani went to talk with the guard on the right, while Tristan was called to the left.

"Name and destination." The guard didn't even bother to look up.

"Trevor Calloway and Darryl Morningstar. I don't know our destination."

Darryl chose that moment to let out a scream.

The guard, no longer bored, looked at them more closely. "Let me scan your IDs."

Darryl squirmed and fussed until a second guard came over to help.

"Right," she said, sitting back at her desk. "Now your destination?"

"I don't know. My uncle is taking me on a surprise trip for my birthday."

Darryl squirmed until he got out of Tristan's grasp and ran to Techani, who was just about to pass through the gate.

"Sorry about that." Tristan got up to go get the boy.

The guard rose too. "You're clear to go. Happy birthday."

"Thank you." Tristan bowed to her just a little and hurried to catch up with Darryl and Techani.

Darryl was giggling at the funny faces Techani made for him.

"What was all that about?" Techani asked.

Tristan shrugged.

This side of the gate had no shops. The walls were lined with travel posters showing happy families enjoying resorts on different worlds. There were security gates into the terminals at regular intervals. They walked in silence until they came to the last gate.

This one scared Tristan the most. He had to walk into the booth with Darryl and hope that the body scan wouldn't reveal who he was. In all the vids, this was the part where people were caught, or the doors didn't open, or something horrible happened. He didn't breathe until the door on the other side opened. Techani stepped out a few moments later.

When they were strapped into their seats, Tristan was ready to relax.

"What happened back there?" Techani asked. "At the second gate."

So much for relaxing. "I don't know. Darryl just started screaming."

"Did you notice anything about the guard?"

Tristan tried to think. She was a thin woman with a heavy chest. Her red hair was pulled back under her uniform cap. "I can't think of anything out of the ordinary."

Techani nodded. "And what do you make of Darryl's reaction?"

"He's such a happy boy. He smiles at anyone who smiles at him. She wasn't smiling exactly, but she wasn't making scary faces either." Tristan looked over at the boy who was happily playing with the rubber ring they'd given him earlier.

Darryl noticed them looking and dropped the toy and giggled. Tristan picked it up and handed it back to him.

"Ba ba ba ba," Darryl said and threw the toy again.

"What do you think?" Tristan asked.

Techani laughed. "You aren't as dense as your tutors like to complain."

Tristan rolled his eyes.

"I think it was just one of those things, but we'll have to watch carefully if it happens again."

"Why?"

"Kids notice things in different ways. Sometimes that makes them smarter than adults."

Tristan sighed and leaned back. He tried to relax.

CHAPTER FOUR

MURPHY - TRANSFER STATION

Murphy didn't understand why a shuttle flight couldn't have net access. Six hours of sitting staring at his disabled tablet would be enough to drive anyone over the edge. Add the anxiety of not hearing back from Emalynn. All he'd heard from Tabby and Claire was acknowledgment of Emalynn's flight information. She should have docked before his flight turned off the net. Six hours of worry made him wonder if the station would even be there.

He toggled his tablet on as soon as the shuttle connected to the docking tube. Still nothing. He ran into several people while trying to see if there was something wrong with the tablet itself. It wasn't until he ran into a door that refused to open that he realized he would need to hire a room on the station. In the room he would have even greater access to station systems, to find where Tabby and Claire were hiding. He dropped his bag on the bed and booted up the in-room terminal.

"What are you looking for today?" Happy bright-red letters asked in the middle of the screen while icons for food, entertainment, exercise, and people popped up in the corners.

Murphy tapped the people icon and entered Emalynn's name.

"Sorry, there is no one registered by that name at this time." This time the letters were green. They still looked too happy for Murphy's mood.

"Tabby Darichron is located in the health wing. No further information available." When Murphy entered her name, this information materialized in purple.

"Claire Yevet is located in the health wing. No further information is available." Also in purple.

He couldn't imagine what project they could be working

on that would have them in the health wing. Then he never really understood what they did. He ignored the knots in his chest as he headed out.

"How can I help you?" asked the nurse at the admissions desk. He looked Murphy up and down as though running a medical scan. Maybe he was.

"I'm looking for my friends, Tabby and Claire. Tabby Darichron and Claire Yevet. They are working on a project—"

The man didn't wait for Murphy to finish talking before looking down at the screen.

"I'm sorry, neither of them has woken up yet." He did sound genuinely sorry. "What did you say your relationship was?"

"Friend. They aren't expecting me." Murphy couldn't draw a full breath.

"Please have a seat." The nurse smiled as he waved to the waiting room.

Murphy chose a seat where he would be able to see as many of the doors as possible. He tried to call Emalynn again, but her tablet didn't respond. He left yet another message to call him and looked up to see a solid woman in a security uniform standing in front of him.

"Murphy Sanchain?"

"Yes," Murphy squeaked. He couldn't deny that things had gone bad anymore.

"We'd like to ask you a few questions." "We" included another equally solid woman standing near the exit.

Murphy nodded.

"You may use the consultation room." The nurse offered.

The guards ushered Murphy into a sterile room with a simple table bolted to the floor and five chairs designed to be uncomfortable. Murphy took the chair farthest from the door. The pretty one, who'd greeted him, sat down opposite him. The other, with features too small for her face and muscles to make up for it, stayed by the door. They both looked at him. Not mean, not stern, just eyes peering deep beyond his skin.

"I was just trying to find my friends," Murphy started. "I knew they were on the station for some kind of project. They aren't expecting me or anything."

"Slow down, son." The pretty one raised her hands in a calming gesture. "We know you didn't do anything. We're investigating an incident."

Murphy clamped his mouth shut. Confusion and fear

made it hard to figure out what was going on.

"We just need to know a little more about them." The second guard spoke with soft tones.

"Why? What happened?"

"That's what we're trying to find out. So tell us what you know about them."

Murphy swallowed hard. He never trusted authorities, but he had to say something. "Tabby is an investigator. She does documentary stuff. She never tells anyone other than Claire what she's working on until it's released. Claire's her partner and film crew." That was the part they could verify with a quick net search. Their work with his parents was secret.

"So what were they doing here and in the cargo loading bays?"

Murphy saw the test in her question. "I told you... They don't talk about their projects."

"No, you only said that about Tabby."

"Well, it's Tabby's project. And before you ask, they told me they were coming because they knew I was staying with my aunt and would probably love a visit from someone familiar."

"So why are you staying with your aunt?" The guard leaned in close. "So close to graduation and you've been transferred six times."

"I thought you wanted to know about Tabby and Claire." And how did she know that about him?

The guards glanced at each other. "You're a smart kid. Just tell us what you're hiding."

Murphy clamped his mouth shut again. He was off his game. He could out silence them if he had to, even with both of them staring at him. They'd already admitted that he hadn't done anything, so they wouldn't be able to hold him.

"Ms. Yevet is awake." The nurse interrupted. "She's asking for him."

"This should be interesting, then," said the lead guard. "Come with us."

They all followed the nurse through the waiting room into another sterile corridor, past several rooms, until he stopped at an open door. Claire had a black eye so swollen her eyelids were hidden. When she saw Murphy, she tried to sit up against all the wires and tubes.

"What the hell were you thinking? That girl is a total psycho."

Murphy tried to back away. The guard behind him put a

hand on his shoulder to hold him there.

"Ms. Yevet, do you know who attacked you?" asked the lead guard.

"His girlfriend. He sent her up here to get away from her mother's murderer. You never told us *she* was the murderer. You said she's a cheerleader."

"Calm down, Ms. Yevet." The guard shot a look at her partner. "What's her name?"

"Emalynn something."

"Emalynn Algrian?"

"Yeah, that's it. Stupid kid. What the hell were you thinking?"

The nurses shooed them away and gave Claire a shot that put her back to sleep.

Back in the hall, the guards turned on Murphy. "So, tell us about Emalynn Algrian."

#

TRISTAN - SANTA ANNA LUXURY LINER

Tristan lounged on the couch in their suite on the Santa Anna Luxury Liner. It was a step up from the hotel they'd been staying in. For one thing, they each had a separate sleeping room, including Darryl. The other was that they'd managed to buy enough travel toys for Darryl that he had something to do when he wasn't napping. The other major improvement was that Techani had gotten him a new ID so he would be able to leave the suite when it got too small for him.

While it was a step up from the hotel, he still missed the royal transport. His rooms there were larger than this whole suite, and they were set up exactly the way he liked them. The bed here, though comfortable, was softer than he liked, and none of the pillows quite fit his head. His wardrobe was disturbingly limited as well, but that could be fixed in time. Now that he was allowed to choose his own clothes, the options were overwhelming. The hardest thing to get used to was the open net. Even the research sites contradicted each other about just about everything. How was he supposed to know what was real and what was propaganda?

"What are you doing here?" Techani startled Tristan. "I thought you would be anywhere other than our rooms after the last week."

Tristan shrugged. "I guess I got used to it."

"I doubt that." Techani moved Tristan's feet so he could sit on the far end of the couch. "What are you researching today?"

"I'm trying to trace the resources for this report about ungraduateds going to live among the Others." Tristan poked at another link leading to yet another of the news sites. "It just can't be right, but all the sources appear to be legitimate."

"What makes you doubt it?"

Tristan sat up to see the expression on his protector's face. Techani looked serious, with not even a hint of a joke in his eyes. "It can't be right. The only people who don't graduate are those who are incapable of passing the tests. They wouldn't be able to do what the article said they would."

"I see." Techani took the tablet from Tristan and read for a moment. "What is it that makes a person incapable of passing the tests?"

"If they can't learn."

"What causes that?"

Tristan glowered at Techani. "You aren't one of my tutors."

"But I'm all you've got, so humor me." Techani flashed him a smile. "What causes people to be unable to learn?"

"Brain damage... Some are just born stupid... I don't know." Tristan fell back on the arm of the couch.

"Anything else?"

"Stupid teachers."

Techani didn't say anything.

"What? Are you going to tell me there are no stupid teachers?"

"Not at all." He was back to looking serious. "Think about it. If a student were cursed with even one stupid teacher, would they be able to graduate?"

"Yes... No... I don't know." Tristan didn't like where this was leading.

"What about students who are denied teachers?"

"That can't happen. The law says that all students must be taught."

"And everyone always follows the law."

Tristan almost said "yes" but caught the fallacy before it left his mouth. "But who would do that to their children? It would mean they'd never be citizens." Even as he said it, he knew. Not all children had parents. There were laws about orphans. And corporations were notorious for skipping the laws they didn't like. "That just sucks."

Techani nodded. "I think you're going to learn a lot more than your parents expected on this trip."

"Are you saying that all this was planned?" He couldn't believe that.

Techani laughed. "You mean blowing up your ship and losing a couple hundred valuable staff in the process? No, that wasn't part of the plan. Letting you go to the mall, getting you away from your handlers so you have a chance to meet friends your mother won't approve of—that was the plan."

Tristan stared at the man hired to protect him. "But Mother hired you."

"And your father added this bit to my mission, but don't tell your mother." Techani reached over and squeezed Tristan's shoulder. "Now you know. What do you want to do about it?"

The possibilities flooded Tristan's mind. They could join one of the research groups studying the Others. He could go to high school. He could try out for a cheer squad just like... "I want to find my sister."

"You don't have a sister." Techani looked about as skeptical as any other adult Tristan had told about his sister.

"That's what they say, but I know—I have a twin sister."

"How do you know?"

"I just know."

Techani sighed. "Why do you, whose life has been documented second by second from birth 'til now, think that you have a sister for whom there is no record?"

"I went looking for the records in the archives, but my birth isn't there." Tristan smirked at Techani. "There are three days of records that are just missing. We don't even know for sure who was there, other than Mother. And"—he held up a hand to stop Techani from interrupting—"that means there is no way to prove me wrong, or right."

"And nothing to suggest another baby."

"There was a trial." Tristan sat up. Finally someone willing to listen. "It was hard to dig up the records, and they're encrypted even in the royal system, but I was able to find some parts. I figured out that someone tried to kill Mother during the birth. There was one nurse who said, 'After that, the prince was born.' It doesn't make a lot of sense, but after what? I also know that if there are twins, one will always be a girl and the other a boy and the girl is born first eighty percent of the time."

Tristan flopped back on the couch to stare at the ceiling. "I went looking because of the dreams. Almost nightly, I dream I'm a girl, living a very different life, but it's not me. You know how dreams are. It's not me remembering the fear of a raid or the joy of winning a cheer competition. When I was little, I told my nurses about the dreams and they laughed."

Techani had sat up during Tristan's speech, and there was something new in his gaze. "To think that Master Grishan swears you are incapable of paying attention. Well, let's just say you've convinced me to a point."

"I know it sounds crazy... Wait, you believe me?"

"Enough to let you lead the search. Where should we start?"

Tristan could see the skepticism in Techani's eyes. "You just want a random path."

"Proving your masters wrong again." Techani smiled. "True, and following a crazy investigation that no one else will think of gives us that."

Tristan flopped back again. "I knew it."

"Hey, just because I don't believe doesn't mean you're wrong."

Tristan opened and closed his mouth three times before he found the words. "Thank you."

#

EMALYNN - A STOREROOM

Emalynn woke in a dark place. It took a moment to put her dreams aside and remember where she was.

"Where are you?" The voice startled her.

She held her breath, hoping to stay hidden.

"Where are you?" It came from everywhere and nowhere at the same time.

Emalynn thought she recognized the voice.

"Where are you?"

"Shut up," she whispered.

"Where are you?"

She clamped her hands over her ears, only to find the voice was in her head.

Go away! She huddled in her little space until the voice stopped.

Enough time had passed that she should be able to slip back into the main stream. She pushed the small crate just enough to slip out of the hidey-hole. Each step echoed through the room. *Everything is fine. I'm just going to slip back out and be on my way.* She didn't believe herself.

The door whooshed open onto an empty corridor. The knots in Emalynn's stomach tightened as she walked to the airlock. It was sealed. Emalynn stared at the stars through the tiny window. *Crud and double crud. No worse than that, crap.*

She was sure to be noticed now that she'd opened one door. That gave her maybe a minute to plan. She wouldn't be able to fight her way out of this, and hiding was no longer an option. That left her with the truth or a really good story.

The sound of another door whooshing open ended her chance to come up with a good story. She stayed right where she was, staring out the airlock window.

"Don't move," the larger of the two women commanded. They were dressed in serviceable brown security uniforms. The tall one had short black hair over dark skin while the shorter had red hair pulled back tight over skin so light it looked white.

"Who are you and what are you doing here?" the smaller woman asked.

Emalynn concentrated on breathing and not panicking.

"Who are you?" The shorter one stepped forward with her weapon raised.

"Emalynn, my name is Emalynn." Now she was going to have to tell the truth. Emalynn kicked herself for not having a story ready.

"What are you doing here?"

Emalynn glanced back at the airlock before answering. "I didn't know I was off the station."

The taller woman laughed. "How do you miss going through an airlock?"

Emalynn shrugged.

"Liar." The short woman growled, but she let the tip of her weapon fall. "Right, then, come with us."

The taller woman holstered her stunner and grabbed Emalynn's arm. Emalynn let the woman half drag and half push her down the corridor. She didn't resist when they shoved her into the lift either, though she had to bite back a nasty comment. She'd met guards like this before—more worried about their own power than doing things properly. Knowing they were bullies made it easier to keep to the meek act as they pushed and prodded her into the brig, a white room with a control desk in the middle and five cells around the outside. Prisoners would have a hard time seeing each other, but the controller would be able to watch them easily.

They pushed her into the middle cell. Emalynn had hoped they would leave her some privacy, but no. Emalynn sat on the bench of the cell and listened to the women laugh about her situation. They were certain that Chief Lane was going to have a lark with her. Captain Barosa would find it all quite silly too. Their laughter was cut short when two more women joined them.

The one dressed in a well-decorated brown uniform and short blond hair must be the dreaded Chief Lane and the other, also in a well-decorated blue uniform and almond-shaped eyes would be the captain.

"What are you doing on my ship?" the latter one asked, confirming she was the captain.

"I didn't mean to be," Emalynn said. "I just, well, I thought they were going to kill me."

The captain looked at the guards with a sharp expression. "Who was trying to kill you?"

"Not them." Emalynn hated having to defend those two. "These other women. I don't know who they were. I just needed a place to hide for a bit. I'm really sorry. I didn't mean to be here."

The captain looked to the security chief who nodded once.

"Well, you're here. Your parents to pay for your passage?"

"I don't have parents." That brought a chorus of raised eyebrows. How could this get any worse? "My mother was killed yesterday. I panicked and ran. Please don't turn me in."

"You have family?"

Yes, but I don't know who they are. "No."

This elicited another silent exchange between the captain and her chief. Emalynn wished she could ask Baba what to do now. Baba had never shied away from custody when it was to her advantage, but how did you turn a situation like this to your advantage?

"We'll have to verify your story." The chief spoke. Her voice was soft and warm. "Let me scan your ID and tell me now if you've had it hacked."

Emalynn held her hand to the glass of her cell. "I've been hacked, many times."

The chief nodded for the others to leave. She did something on the control panel and the lights changed.

"Tell me what to look for."

Emalynn looked into the woman's eyes and saw only sympathy.

CHAPTER FIVE

MURPHY - STATION BRIG

"Lazy bum." Davy's voice pulled Murphy awake.

"Aw hell."

"Don't talk to me that way. I have to come all the way here to pull my son out of jail again."

Murphy closed his eyes again. "Dad, I'm sorry..."

"Save it for the trip home."

Murphy, as always, watched in awe as Davy managed to pull off his role as father, when in reality he was half a year younger than Murphy. Of course Murphy played his part as the chastised son until they were through all record keeping and out of the detention zone.

"What did you do?"

"You mean besides hack our IDs?" Davy smiled at him. "You're going to want to go in and fix some of that. I made your hack a little obvious."

Murphy resisted the urge to check right then. "Yeah, besides that part."

"Your last report—Baba was confirmed as Genise Shaw. You found the real one. Then you lost her. At least now we know who we're looking for, well, you're looking for. What happened with Tabby and Claire puts you a little in debt, and no one else wants to face her anyway."

Murphy could feel the blush in his cheeks. "I didn't know..."

Davy just shook his head. "I know, but the truth is she's dangerous and she knows you. Find her and bring her back."

They were approaching the security gates for the passenger terminals and had to break off the conversation while they could be easily overheard. What was Emalynn thinking now? Did she even know that the ones she left in the hospital wing were the friends he'd sent to help her? Not to mention where had she gone?

Davy was deep into something on his tablet when Murphy stepped out of the last security scan.

"What now?"

"Here." Davy handed over Murphy's tablet. "I just added the codes that get you access to the special account. Don't spend it all in one place."

Murphy took the tablet and checked the account balance. He almost dropped the tablet when he saw the number. He'd never seen an account that full before.

"Did you see...?"

"Yeah, and I used some to get here in style." Davy smiled again. "Perks are a good thing if you don't overuse them."

Murphy peeked at the usage and saw the first-class express ticket and its price. "Perks are a good thing. Can you imagine the kind of trouble we could get in with this?"

Davy laughed. "I remember the kinds of trouble we got in without it. I tell you those rich kids don't know what they're missing."

"Yeah? What's first class like?" Murphy remembered all the times they'd hitched on the trains to get out of town when they were growing up. Dangerous stuff, more so as a pair of boys. They didn't think about that back then. Still didn't most of the time.

"Boring."

"What?" Murphy caught the sly grin on Davy's face.

"They do everything for you. Like cut the meat, dress the salad, even put your seat back when you want a nap..." He sighed dramatically.

Murphy scowled.

"It was the most comfortable chair I've ever sat in, including Mom's special chair."

"Worth it?"

"We'll see."

"What do you mean?"

"I'm flying coach back home. I guess they're monitoring the account. You're coming with me to Torshen. Then you're on your own."

"What?"

This time Davy wasn't smiling. He turned his tablet so Murphy could read the message from an Alecti Army general:

40

"Return and explain." Followed by an itinerary. Murphy had seen that message before and it never ended well. The army gave them more responsibility than they were ready for and expected more maturity than they had. They did their best to live up to it because the alternative was far more restrictive.

"Don't worry." Davy cleared the message and smiled again. "I'll support you whatever you decide. In it for the win."

"In it for the win." Murphy agreed.

"Just remember one thing. With the assassination, time is short." Davy was serious for moment, then cracked a smile. "But then she's your girlfriend too, so that won't be an issue."

The boarding call came, and they crowded into their coach seats. Conversation turned to catching up on all the gossip.

#

EMALYNN - PTERODACTYL BRIG

Time did funny things in a brig cell. Emalynn had never wished to be in Miss Lackey's history lecture until now. Even the dry recitation of events that didn't have any connection to her life was preferable to absolute nothing. The cell was too small to practice the faster forms, but Tai Chi could be practiced in small places.

"I think I recognize that one." Emalynn jumped when the security chief spoke. Chief Lane and Captain Barosa were watching her.

"Do you want me to start from the beginning?"

The chief nodded. Emalynn felt the slight tightening of her stomach that told her she was performing for a valued audience. She started to move, holding each move to prove her balance as well as displaying her understanding of the form. As always, even with an audience, she relaxed as she progressed.

"Beautiful. Can you use that at full speed?"

"Yes." Emalynn blushed as she remembered the attack just before she hid on the Pterodactyl. She'd used a mix of forms for that.

The chief nodded to the captain. The captain nodded back.

"Open the door," Captain Barosa ordered.

"Are you sure?" the security guard at the controls asked. "You just heard her admit she's dangerous."

The captain nodded. "If she tries anything, we'll space her."

41

The cell door slid aside and Emalynn stepped out. She stood as tall as she could in the face of two powerful women.

"You are a very hard person to trace. Your ID has been hacked more times than I could count. Apparently, you were born at the age of two."

There was no question, so Emalynn kept her mouth shut. What would Baba have done? Baba wouldn't have gotten into this mess.

"I suppose you wouldn't know anything that far back, would you?"

Emalynn took the offered lie and shook her head. "I know that Baba isn't my birth mother, if that's what you are asking."

"She was ungraduated. Why would she care about a child not her own?"

"Because she was ungraduated."

"So you would support her?"

Emalynn shrugged.

The women looked at each other. Emalynn could see the secret language of long association but didn't understand it.

"You said you would work for you passage." The captain asked, "Is that still true?"

She nodded. There was hope yet.

"Good, because I just bought your contract from the state."

Emalynn felt her breath die in her chest.

"What? How?"

"You were classed an orphan, but since you weren't deliverable, I was able to talk down your price to only ten thousand."

"Ten thousand? That's all I'm worth?"

"That's all you owe. Far less than a week's stay on board as a passenger."

She was in debt before graduation. Emalynn stumbled back and sat hard on the bench of her cell.

Captain Barosa sat next to her. "It's hard to learn that you are a debt. Every orphan learns it. Now you can do one of two things about it. Worry about it until it kills you or let it motivate you to work it off."

"Baba worked so hard to prevent this."

"She did a fabulous job."

"But I got bought. That's exactly what she didn't want."

"She wanted you to be a citizen. You still have three years to graduate, and if you think I'm going to let it take that long, you're going to be in for a surprise."

Emalynn looked up in shock. She saw the grin and sparkling eyes of the security chief first, then the softer expression on the captain's face.

"Only ten thousand credits? What jobs do you have available?"

The women laughed.

"I told you," the chief said. "Time to think and she'd get there."

"I owe you." Captain Barosa turned back to Emalynn. "I need an assistant. Someone smart, resourceful, and capable of keeping herself out of trouble."

"Or I could use a security trainee. She would need to be strong, dependable, and capable of defending herself and our guests." The chief offered.

They were both tempting offers. "Who pays more?"

The women laughed again. "They both pay twenty credits per week. There will be no charge for your room and board. And you will complete all your studies."

It would take her ten years to earn her freedom. She'd be too old to graduate after the contract. "Will there be opportunities to earn more?"

The women laughed again. "And it's even," the captain said. "Yes, there will be some opportunities, but don't count on them."

She knew the work of security for the most part. "What would I do for you, Captain?"

Chief Lane smiled and held up a finger to the captain.

The captain ignore her. "Pretty much whatever I tell you to, including greeting guests, making coffee, and perhaps taking a bridge shift if you are capable."

"I think I'd rather be your assistant, Captain."

The chief smiled. "Well, let's get you into your quarters, then. You'll begin your duties tomorrow. You have a lot of studying to do."

Emalynn followed the chief through the maze of corridors, trying to get an idea of where they were. The best she could tell, they were heading toward the bow, where the bridge would be.

"Here." The chief stopped by a door like every other they had passed. Inside was a room about twice the size of the cell, with a real bed and desk. There was a terminal on the desk. "The captain's quarters are the next door up. Showers are the fourth on the left down that way."

"I have a question," Emalynn blurted when the chief

turned to leave. "Why did Captain Barosa do this for me?"

The chief came back into the little cabin far enough for the door to close behind her.

"Rosa is a lot like your Baba, except she was one of the lucky ones. Her corporation allowed her to graduate but left her with a stifling debt. She found a way to buy herself out. She has a soft spot for orphans. Most of the crew are, and some of them even managed to graduate. We are very loyal."

Emalynn acknowledged the threat in the chief's words.

#

TRISTAN - SANTA ANNA STATEROOM

"I found her." Tristan dropped to the floor next to Techani who was meditating again. "I know where my sister is. You aren't going to believe it."

Techani cracked one eye open.

"She's on the Pterodactyl. Here, look." He pushed his tablet into Techani's hands with the brochure for the luxury cruiser open.

Techani took the tablet and opened his eyes all the way. "I've seen this."

"What have I been telling you every morning?"

Techani nodded.

"Then look right there." Tristan pointed to the grand ballroom. "Last night, I saw her there with the crest in full view."

"Good, it's on our itinerary." Techani flipped the screen on the tablet over to their schedule. "Yup, we transfer on board in a month."

"A month? Can we transfer sooner?" Tristan tried not to look too pathetic.

Techani gave him a look. "I don't think so, but I will try."

Tristan nearly bounced out of his chair. "Thank you. Thank you, thank you, thank you."

"What are you going to do if she's not there?" Techani's voice of reason burst into his wild fantasy.

"She is there."

"Okay, let's assume you're right and she's there right now. It'll be at least a week before this ship gets to a station. We'll hire an express, which will still take week to catch up with the Pterodactyl. What happens if she leaves in that time?"

Tristan wanted to deny that could happen, but he'd

known all along that her life changed often.

"It's just a start. We could pick up her trail." Just like the vids. "Someone will know where she's gone."

"You're just going to walk up to the captain and ask if your sister was there and where she went?"

Tristan glared at his guardian. "You're making this too complicated."

"Nonsense." Techani stretched as he got up. "I'm just getting you to think of all the possibilities."

Tristan watched Darryl playing with a strange collection of things they'd given him. How simple the boy's life was. All he had to worry about was finding enough things to play with.

Darryl noticed the attention and crawled over to Tristan. "Go-go?"

"Not right now." Tristan pulled the boy into his lap. "We have to wait."

"Go Mama." Darryl poked at Tristan's chest.

"We are going to find my sister."

Darryl shook his head. "Ma ma ma." He squirmed down to the floor and toddled about the room singing, "Ma ma ma."

Tristan sighed. "The Pterodactyl is a public company, right? We could look at their records. Maybe we could find her that way."

"Good thinking, but the Pterodactyl is a private ship."

"Isn't there a way to find out who works for them?"

Techani sighed. "Not legally."

Tristan groaned. "With all the laws that have been broken already, does it really matter?"

Techani lowered his eyebrows.

"I mean, is it okay to break the law if it means setting something right?"

"Now you are getting to the heart of the matter. People have been struggling with that question since laws came into existence. I don't think anyone has come to a definite position on that question."

"That's not a helpful answer."

"I never said it was. History is filled with people who have decided on both sides of the issue. You could research the question if you want. It's something to keep you busy."

"You are the most annoying tutor I have ever had."

Techani smiled. "Good thing I'm not your tutor, then."

Tristan grabbed his tablet and flopped back on the couch. He opened a new window into the net. How could he even phrase the question to get a good answer?

"Oh, and since I'm not your tutor, you may want to look up net-based courses to finish your education. You wouldn't want to lose your citizenship because you can't pass the grad tests."

Tristan scowled at Techani and opened yet another window.

CHAPTER SIX

EMALYNN - PTERODACTYL

"I was paged?" Emalynn asked as she walked onto the bridge.

The main view screen showed a small cargo ship angling in for orbit around a large brown planet. Emalynn recognized the Physics of Navigation simulation at once.

"Now you have to see this." Trace, ship navigator, pointed to the little cargo ship as it angled in for final approach. "Odd gravity... and..."

The ship bounced a bit but managed to maintain trajectory, falling into orbit as though nothing had happened. Just the way Emalynn had calculated. The ship's officers all broke out into applause. Emalynn inched back toward the door.

"That puts her four days ahead of expectations and three ahead of the record." Tom reported from the communications station. "She'd have to really screw up to come up short on the last leg."

"Look at the fuel gage." Genevieve pointed to the upper left of the screen. The gage read three-quarters full with a two percent usage. "That can't be right." She pulled out her tablet to run her own calculations

Adda from engineering turned to her panel and tapped in a few characters. "She's running that ship fully loaded and check out the Gees she gives the passengers on that last little trick." She threw an overlay up on the screen.

"Are you sure?" Gretta did her own calculations and threw them up beside Adda's. They showed the same thing. Emalynn's run had kept the tolerances well below standard.

"Can you get better than an A+?" Trace asked. "I've never seen scores like this."

"How real is the simulation?" Captain Barosa asked.

"The physics are real, but there are challenges that you won't find out here. Like the odd gravity."

"So you have to be better than a professional pilot to make it through that course?" The captain turned to catch Emalynn's eye.

"Yeah. A good grade is one where you don't lose the whole crew. Maybe one student a generation makes it through the course fully intact."

"Did she cheat?"

Trace looked at the captain and followed her eyes to Emalynn. "Not that I can tell. She got creative, but the simulation is supposed to handle that. Like using the gravity generators to counter a hard turn. Not a cheat, and I'm sure this is going to get out to all the Nav centers."

"Lock it down." The captain turned back to Trace.

"Captain?"

"That simulation was never turned in. Don't. Not until you can be sure there was no cheating, and that means understanding everything she did."

Trace swallowed hard before acknowledging the order.

"The final approach," Genevieve called. A large star station appeared on the screen. The little ship approached, slowing to match rotation with the station, except it didn't slow quite enough. Emalynn flinched even before the error showed, a jarring impact that everyone on the little ship would have felt.

Tom threw the final stats up on the screen. "Even with the deduction for that final approach, she still beats the standing record by two days."

The crew cheered, some of them jumping up from their chairs. Captain Barosa wore a broad smile. Emalynn wanted to find a hole to crawl into. It was bad enough that she'd been bought off the state, becoming a slave for all practical purposes, but they had to take her schoolwork and show it like an entertainment vid. So what if she got the best score of her generation? The captain just locked it down. And it wouldn't go into her grade anyway. How had they even found it? What else had they scanned? *Do I have any privacy?*

"Congratulations." Genevieve pulled her into a hug. "That officially makes you amazing."

Gretta joined the hug. "So have you chosen a specialization yet? Your contract just got a lot more valuable."

"I'm not for sale." Emalynn didn't mean to snap at the

woman.

"I didn't mean it that way. But really, you should be a Navigations apprentice."

Emalynn wasn't ready to forgive yet. "I have things to do."

She wasn't ready to forgive the contract or the captain in forcing her into it. Only the fact that she was treated as a member of the crew kept the sting to a manageable level. She turned to leave.

"Emalynn, stand fast," Chief Lane ordered.

Emalynn stopped in her tracks but didn't turn around. "We have a supply run at the next station and passengers boarding in the morning. I have to be ready for them."

There was silence behind her. She refused to turn to see what was happening.

"Your schedule is clear until Chief Lane tells me otherwise," Captain Barosa said.

Emalynn nodded her acceptance.

"With me." Chief Lane passed her.

Emalynn scrambled to catch up. They walked in silence for a few halls.

"What's so interesting about your current duties that you don't want to take an apprenticeship for your contract?"

Emalynn winced at the mention of the contract. "Nothing." There was silence again. "It's just, I want to do what I have to and get on with my life."

The chief stopped, pulling Emalynn up short. "You did notice that clause in your contract that you are still a high school student?"

"Yeah."

"And students are supposed to be looking for internships."

"I know."

"So why don't you want to be a navigation apprentice?"

Emalynn examined the toes of her shoes. She did want to be a navigator. That's what she'd planned. "It's the passengers."

The chief laughed. "Passengers? You mean the ones who treat us all like their personal slaves and we have to just keep smiling? That's what's keeping you from following your dreams?"

"I..."

"If you weren't dreaming of being a navigator, you should." The chief continued their walk. "Which passengers are you referring to?"

Emalynn jogged a few steps to catch up again. "The ones joining us tomorrow morning."

Chief Lane pulled up her tablet. "Ah, yes, Techani Kenchi, Trevor Calloway, and Darryl Morningstar."

"Just Techani Kenchi." Under the chief's questioning look, she continued. "My mother talked of her master fondly. She always said if I was alone, I should find him. I'm hoping he is the right one, but it's hard to tell through the hacks in his profile."

They'd arrived at one of the crew gyms. Chief Lane chased the two guards sparring out. She flipped the switch that shut off the cameras. "What do you mean about hacks?"

Emalynn pulled up the profile and its meta table. "There, there, and there. Why were those edits made? He's been private security for the royals for years, so why was there a hacked change to his employment a month ago? If you didn't see the hack, you'd think he worked for the Calloways all that time."

The chief took the tablet to stare even closer at the information. "I'm supposed to convince you to sign on as a navigation apprentice with Gretta, but I'm tempted to take you as a security apprentice."

Emalynn stamped her foot in frustration.

"All right, what's going on?"

Emalynn slowly turned her eyes back to the chief. All she saw was concern. With a deep breath, she explained how Baba had warned Emalynn to never get into this kind of situation. "I know it's silly."

"It's not silly. I know what it's like to have only your pride. I'm one of the unlucky ones here. Captain Barosa didn't find me in time to graduate. So is Gretta."

"It's not just pride. I failed. Baba taught me how to use the systems so I wouldn't be here working for my freedom. And now... I don't even know who I am anymore. You aren't helping any."

The older woman put the tablet aside and grabbed Emalynn by the shoulders. Emalynn knocked her hands away. When the chief just laughed, Emalynn launched her own attack, which was blocked. They sparred until Emalynn didn't have enough energy to be angry anymore. The chief looked just as exhausted.

"Feel better?"

Emalynn nodded.

"Good, so will you be an apprentice?"

Emalynn looked away.

"At this point, any of the crew would be happy to take you on. And you'll still have time to contact Master Kenchi."

Emalynn thought about it while she pulled her breath back to normal. "I'll apprentice to Adda."

"Not Gretta?"

Emalynn shook her head. "The captain asked Adda to check for cheating."

The chief smiled and nodded.

#

MURPHY - CABRILE STATION

Murphy narrowed his search for Emalynn to two ships— the Pterodactyl cruise liner and the Oxbow cargo hauler. With nothing else to go on, he chose to track down the Oxbow first. It's what he would have done—big ship, small crew would make it easier to hide. He booked an express flight to the Cabrile mining station and started making plans for how to break the news to Ly. Of course, he'd have to calm her down after her ordeal, but he knew just how to sweet-talk her in that way.

Murphy got to Cabrile with just enough time to set himself up as an inspector before the Oxbow docked. He had to bribe his way through several layers of officials to get access to the docking bay. He struck an officious pose seconds before the captain disembarked.

"Captain Davies." Murphy stepped forward even before the dock master had a chance to greet the captain. "I need to inspect your ship for a fugitive."

Captain Davies was a large woman who looked like she could break Murphy in two with one hand. The expression on her face as she turned to him made that possibility seem likely.

"You dare suggest that I could have a stowaway on my ship without noticing?"

Murphy smiled. "Because the girl I'm looking for is not your average stowaway." He turned his tablet to the captain with the vid of Emalynn attacking Tabby and Claire.

Captain Davies's expression changed from amusement to horror. "That's what you think is on my ship? Why didn't you prevent this?"

"They were sent to prevent this."

"Are you crazy?" Davies looked him up and down. "You are going to go after her?"

Murphy swallowed the insult. He couldn't afford to back this woman into a corner right now. "I'm not crazy. I'm a friend

51

she'll listen to."

"Eh... It's your life." She waved the rest of her crew to back off.

Murphy spent four hours searching the ship for any sign that Emalynn had ever been there. He even hacked the ship's core systems to look for unusual resource usage. Nothing, not one little thing, to show that there was even a rat more than the five crewmembers listed on the manifest. Four hours to prove to himself that he'd been an idiot.

He slunk out of the ship and back to his little room to track down the Pterodactyl. It had gone in the opposite direction and stopped in six ports. The official site also suggested several shuttle services that could join the cruise between ports, for an additional fee.

"Damn." He slammed his fist into the wall. The pain brought tears to his eyes. He thought better of kicking anything; he didn't need to break a toe as well. He headed for the medical wing.

While sitting in the waiting room, he tried to book another express shuttle. Not a chance. This wasn't a regular stop, and the one he'd come in on already left. In fact, there wouldn't be another passenger shuttle this way for a week. There were three cargo ships seeking crewmembers, but he didn't qualify.

"This rots," he muttered as he closed the connection.

"Got a problem, son?" An old woman sitting next to him asked. She was a little less beat up than most of the miners he'd seen on base.

"I just missed the last shuttle to someplace more populated."

She nodded. "That does rot. You could sign on to another ship."

Murphy snorted. "I'm not the kind of body the cargo ships are looking for."

"You're a hacker, then." She leaned back in her chair, cradling her left arm.

"I didn't say that."

"Didn't have to. Only one reason a kid your size would be out and about. You're trouble. The only kind of trouble that can't hop a freighter is a hacker."

Murphy didn't follow the logic, but she got the right answer.

She laughed again. "Sign with me. Once you get that hand fixed."

"But I don't have skills…"

"You got the ones I'm looking for."

The realization that he was talking to a pirate dawned slowly in Murphy's mind. Murphy hesitated just a moment while she watched him with lidded eyes. "What are the terms?"

"Shrewd, I like that." She sat up and was all business. "You give me and my crew new IDs and we take you wherever you need to go—direct."

"Anywhere?"

"Anywhere at all. We don't got a set schedule, if you catch my star."

He was saved from answering by the nurse calling him in.

"Dock 81." She called just before the clinic door closed behind him. This was just too good to be true, but what could be the harm?

#

TRISTAN - PTERODACTYL

Darryl toddled across the access tube to the Pterodactyl, giggling the whole way. Tristan followed feeling just as happy to be here. Even Techani was having difficulty hiding his smile. Tristan couldn't wait to begin his search for his sister. He had spent most of the last week imagining all the steps he could take to find her. And there she was, smiling at them from the access port, dressed in a spotless blue-and-white uniform.

"Welcome to the Pterodactyl. You must be Techani Kenchi, Trevor Calloway, and Darryl Morningstar?"

"We are and you are…" Tristan almost said "my sister" but shut his mouth, leaving the impression of a question.

"I'm Emalynn. I will be your host and liaison to Captain Barosa." She bowed. "If you need anything during your travels with us, just let me know."

"Ma ma." Darryl held his hands up at Emalynn.

She smiled down at the boy. "Welcome to you too." She looked back up at Tristan with a question just behind her eyes. "I'll show you to your suite."

She led them through the corridors of the liner, pointing out the internal navigation system and other ship attractions. She matched her pace to Darryl's uneven steps. Darryl followed Emalynn, babbling, "Ma ma ma." He let none of the usual distractions turn him from his course.

"Here you are." She palmed her way through the door. The suite was larger than they'd been staying in recently but smaller than he was used to.

"You will need to activate your palm readers to lock your room. You can set your privacy settings from there. We have activated the lower palm pads in case of emergency. You can set Darryl's access levels from this terminal. Once you've activated the palm reader here, you will be recognized throughout the ship."

"Ma ma ma." Darryl held his hands up to Emalynn.

She crouched down to be at his level. "Come here, sweetie. We'll get you registered. Can you put your hand right here?" She used gestures to help Darryl understand.

Darryl did as she said but pulled away his hand too quickly.

"Try again. How long can you hold it there?"

He did it again, holding his hand in place until the door chimed. Emalynn quickly typed in his ID and the door swished open.

"That's it. Now if you get lost, we'll be able to find you. If your papa lets you, you can even follow the shining lights to the playroom. We have about four other kids just your age right now."

Darryl was just eating up all the attention she gave him.

"And the best part is you won't be able to get through any doors that you aren't supposed to. Your papa and uncle can pick and chose from the terminal inside the room since you are registered as a minor. Isn't that just shiny?"

"Ma ma ma." Darryl agreed.

"You can register your palms on either pad." Emalynn stood again. "Master Kenchi, if you would register yours as well, I can leave you to get settled. We'll see you at dinner."

Something passed between Emalynn and Techani, too fast and too subtle for Tristan to catch.

"Ma ma ma." Darryl grabbed her pant leg and pulled her deeper into the room. "Pa pa pa." He reached for Tristan too.

Tristan picked Darryl up in a big hug. "Thank you for all your help."

"It's my pleasure." Her eyes lingered on him for a moment. "If you need me, just hit the blue button on any palm pad."

She backed out of the room and the door slid shut.

"Ma ma ma ma," Darryl cried, struggling out of his arms.

Tristan looked over to Techani who was also staring at the

door.

"What are you thinking?"

"That I haven't been called master in a long time. What about you?"

Tristan turned back to the door. Looking at Emalynn was like looking in a mirror, but it was more than just that. He knew, from the feel of her eyes on his face to the way she smiled.

"Did you see her? I can't believe how easy it was to find her. And now I know her name. Emalynn. It's a beautiful name."

"Breathe."

Tristan started breathing in the slow, deep way that Techani had taught him. He managed three full breaths. "You did see her, right?"

"Yes, I saw Emalynn. She was right there."

"She's my sister."

Techani gave him a hard look. "You are sure? You know how many Tristan lookalikes there are?"

Tristan shot a glare at his protector. "They try to match my style. She didn't."

"Calm yourself." Techani lowered himself onto the couch. "What do you know of your sister?"

"I..." Tristan couldn't really say. "She was a cheerleader before, but something bad happened just after the bombing."

"And how do you know this?"

He dropped to the floor. "I don't know." He explained how he just had to think of her and the images would come. At night, he dreamed of her life. It was too consistent to be fake. He knew it in his heart.

"Then she would know this too?"

Tristan shrugged. He'd never thought of that.

"Then before you get all excited, be sure. Talk to her about it."

"Ma ma. Ahm ahm ahm ly," Darryl put in.

Techani laughed. "All I'm saying is get to know her before telling her she's the princess. Become her friend first. Then we'll see."

It was hard to accept that Techani was right. At least he'd been willing to come here. They had a month-long passage on the luxury liner to give him time.

"I'll take Darryl to the play room." Tristan headed for the door. "And I'll remember to introduce myself as Trevor."

"Remember to breathe."

Tristan nodded as he palmed open the door. Darryl raced

ahead as though he knew where they were going. Tristan took the few minutes to access the guide to the play area. Blue lights flashed along the hall, showing the direction.

Darryl stopped to play with the lights for a few seconds, then followed them down the hall. He squealed with joy when he saw the play zone. The child-height palm reader opened the door for him this time, eliciting a spasm of giggles. The door closed before he could go through. He palmed it open again and nearly shook himself right off his feet. Tristan stuck his foot in the door to prevent it closing again until Darryl went inside.

The room was designed with small children in mind. It was filled, top to bottom and side to side, with brightly colored, heavily padded climbing things. There were small rooms nestled among the tubes and ropes with other activities in them. Under it all was a sea of plastic balls. Tristan took Darryl's shoes off before turning him loose in the area. Gravity was lighter here to encourage more play. Tristan went into the parent lounge where he could watch Darryl.

"I still say they shouldn't even look at the order of succession until there has been an official pronouncement," said the father directly across from Tristan. "I mean, they aren't going to tell us if Tristan is just burned and in recovery. That would just invite whoever bombed his transport to bomb the hospital."

"It's been almost two months. It's demoralizing to keep us in the dark about the future of the government," said the older mother to his right.

"What's so uncertain? Tristan wasn't going to take over for a decade at least. There's plenty of time." The young woman across from him didn't look up from her tablet.

"The future of our government has a direct influence on the future of business. We need to be able to plan," the older mother said.

"So make multiple plans. They are going to change anyway." The young woman swept her finger across the screen.

"How so?" asked the young father to his left.

"Long-range plans change frequently, with the shifting of the planets." The young woman finally looked up.

"I think they need to announce the new heir as soon as possible." The older woman sneered at the younger woman.

"How much does the queen matter anyway? The council of lords makes all the decisions and they aren't going anywhere." The young father asked, matching the young woman's attitude.

Tristan listened to the conversation. This was far more

interesting than any lesson about royal politics his tutors had ever come up with.

CHAPTER SEVEN

TRISTAN - PTERODACTYL

"This is impossible," Tristan yelled at his tablet.

"What's impossible?" Techani didn't break his meditation pose.

Tristan held up his tablet. "How am I supposed to learn how to talk to a girl that I want as a friend if all the vids are about talking to girls to start a romance." He'd figured out how to run into Emalynn plenty, but getting a conversation started was something else.

Techani laughed. "You're specifically looking for boys talking to girls?"

"Yeah."

"Try looking for girls talking to girls."

"How's that going to help?"

"Because friendship doesn't care about gender." Techani dropped his pose. "I thought you were talking to her regularly."

Tristan felt the heat in his cheeks. "I only seem to be able to ask her about the ship. What new vids are playing in the theater? What are the dining options? Are there any good observation windows on this trip? That kind of thing."

"All right." Techani stood and stretched a bit. "Why is that all you talk about?"

He blushed even harder. "I..." He didn't know. "I don't know how to talk about anything else."

"Ah, that's a fairly common problem." Techani came to sit on the couch next to Tristan. "I've often thought it should be a class in high school—the art of conversation."

"All the kids on the vids seemed to know how to start conversations just fine."

"They're actors reading lines an adult wrote for them.

Now let's think about your problem."

"Is it a problem?" Now that he'd found her, getting to know her was more of a challenge than he'd thought.

"Are you succeeding in your goal?"

"No."

"Then it's a problem. We just need to find one question you can ask her without getting too embarrassed. Should be pretty simple."

That just made Tristan's cheeks burn. "What makes you think I'm embarrassed?"

"Because you're a teenage boy trying to start a conversation with a teenage girl."

"She's my sister."

"Even worse."

"You aren't helping."

Techani just laughed.

"So a simple question that I won't screw up."

"Exactly."

Tristan flopped back on the couch. "Why is this so complicated?"

"Have you tried asking her what she likes?"

"That would be..." He was going to say "silly." "Great if I knew when to say it."

"Keep it in mind and you'll figure it out." Techani put his hand on Tristan's shoulder in a sympathetic kind of move, then propelled him off the couch. "Why not go out and practice on some of the other passengers?"

"But you said..."

Techani smiled a deadly kind of smile. "Just remember who you are now. It'll be practice in that too."

Tristan headed out to try meeting other passengers as Trevor. It was a lot harder than the vids or Techani made it seem. As the prince, everyone had either recognized him or been introduced to him. As Trevor, he had to start conversations on his own. It rotted. Even more so when Techani started heading off on his own to do "business," leaving Tristan caring for Darryl.

He was moping over his lunch with Darryl in the small dining room when Emalynn walked by his table. Darryl chose that moment to display how done he was with his sandwich. The bit of bread with peanut butter on it hit Emalynn in the forehead.

"You've got quite the throwing arm." She smiled as she handed the sandwich bite back to Darryl. "They taste better when you eat them."

Darryl giggled and crammed the bite into his mouth.

"Did you need anything else?" Emalynn asked Darryl.

"No. I mean. Wait." Tristan took a deep breath. "Can you sit with us for a bit? I mean, Darryl really likes you and he's so much better behaved when you're around, and I'm babbling aren't I?"

She smiled and sat in the chair opposite him. "If this is all it takes to make him behave, I'd be happy to sit with you."

Great. Now what? "So, um, what do you like to do? I mean, when you aren't working."

"I don't get much of a chance around here." She shrugged. "Duty and studies and all that."

"So I'm keeping you from your duties. I'm sorry."

"Actually, keeping you happy is my duty. And this is one of the easier jobs I've had. You wouldn't believe how some think just because they were able to afford to stay for a week, they are the next sun. But I shouldn't be gossiping."

Tristan hoped his blush didn't show too much.

"It's okay, I won't tell."

"Thanks."

"What do you do when you aren't keeping us happy?" Anything to keep her here and talking to him.

"I've been teaching some of the security team martial arts. My..." She closed her mouth and looked away for a moment. "I learned them growing up."

"Really? Would you show me?" That sounded weird. "My uncle is trying to teach me. I haven't learned much yet, but I would love to see a different style." That didn't make it any better.

"Are you available now?" She was looking at her tablet.

"Um, yes. No, I have to take care of Darryl."

Emalynn pushed the last bit of sandwich at the boy. "Bring him along. He won't be in the way."

#

EMALYNN - PTERODACTYL

Emalynn led Trevor and his son to the crew gym. Captain Barosa wouldn't like it; it breaks the illusion. In the passenger gym, there was only an illusion of privacy. Fortunately, the switch for the crew gym was all but labeled.

"This isn't one of the gyms Techani and I have used before," Tristan said. There was just a hint of a shake in his voice.

"It's a crew gym."

She could see the tension building in his shoulders. It was too dangerous to say anything more where they were being recorded. She let them into the gym, big enough for half of security to work out together. Trevor hesitated.

"I'm not going to lock you in. This is probably the safest room on the ship." She smiled at Darryl to get the boy laughing.

Trevor put him down and let him run. "Why here?"

Emalynn touched the secret panel across from the door. The lights shifted just enough to tell her the recordings were stopped.

"We are not being recorded now."

"Are you crazy? That's illegal."

"This is a private ship. We are in a private area. We were recorded coming in and we will be recorded leaving. That's all that the law requires." She hated hiding behind that loophole. "I need to ask something, um, private."

He stood there looking at her as though she were a mirror.

"Your name isn't Trevor, is it?"

His shoulders released.

"Darryl isn't really your son any more than Techani Kenchi is your uncle."

"How...?" He backed up to the wall and slid down. "How can you know that?"

Darryl came between them. "Mama." He hugged her leg. "Baba." He toddled over to Trevor's leg.

"I checked your ID a little deeper than necessary, and it doesn't have much history. Darryl's, however, claims his mother is Marichi Ghehanna, deceased in a mining accident on Prima. Master Kenchi was my mother's teacher. I was supposed to find him if anything happened."

"Well, if you know all that, what more do you need to ask?"

"Your real name. Why you are here? And why do I know you?" Her chest tightened around the fear that he wouldn't answer.

He looked at her as though trying to see through her.

"I'm Prince Tristan." His voice came so soft and tight she almost didn't hear him. "I came looking for you because I believe you are my sister."

She hadn't expected even one of those words. It was her turn to sink to the floor. What had Baba done?

"Sister?" She gasped. It was too crazy, but she couldn't deny it now that he'd said it. "How...?"

"I don't know." He looked up at the cameras in the corners of the room. "You're sure they're off."

She looked at the room lights. They were still in privacy mode. "Positive."

"It's a state secret that the queen's doctor tried to kill her during our birth. For some reason, there are three days of records missing from that time too. I'm not supposed to talk about it, but I know that I have a sister."

If Baba hadn't told her a similar story about the kidnapping, she wouldn't have believed a word he said.

"How do you know you have a sister if no one else does?"

He put his head back against the wall. "How don't you?"

She felt herself making faces as she tried to understand his question.

"I know you because you are in here." He jabbed himself in the chest. "I only have to clear my mind and I know what you're doing. I knew when you won your regional cheer tournament. I felt it when you saw that woman dead. I knew you. I found you here because I thought about you and I could see what you were seeing. Haven't you been able to do the same?"

"You're saying we're twins?" She could hear the shake in her own voice.

Alarms burst through everything. The cameras came back on. While Tristan went to comfort Darryl, Emalynn logged into the ship's system to see what had happened.

Another ship was on a collision course with them. Everything about the other ship screamed pirate, almost as loudly as if they had painted the skull and crossbones on the bow.

"By the stars." Tristan looked over her shoulder. "Pirates! This isn't a coincidence." All color drained out of his face. "I don't have enough protection here."

"I have to go." She took off down the corridors.

"Wait for me." Tristan, carrying Darryl, came running after her.

"No." She put her hand out to stop him. "I'm not a safe person to be around right now."

"I've got nothing."

Panic pressed in against her heart.

"Come on, then." She took Darryl so Tristan could keep up.

She palmed her way into the shuttle bay. That shouldn't have worked. She checked the trajectories again. Good, the other ship was aiming for the bow. She started the auto sequence for shuttle six, then dragged Tristan and Darryl to the smallest of the hopper shuttles.

"Get in and strap in tight."

He strapped himself and Darryl into the copilot's seat. Not where she really wanted them, but there was no time to argue. Any moment someone was bound to notice what she was doing and she needed to get the shuttle bay open before they could stop her.

She sent the signal to the main ship to evacuate the shuttle bay. That would seal the air locks to the ship as well. *Please, please, please, let them be more worried about that ship than us,* she prayed. She finally got the signal that the bay was in vacuum. Now would be the tricky part.

Cut gravity and open the bay doors. She edged the shuttle forward slowly even before the doors were all the way open. This shuttle should fit through at half open, but she didn't trust her skills that much. The shuttle passed through the doors with inches to spare. She reversed the doors as soon as she was out. Anything to make it harder for them to pull her back.

"What do you think you're doing?" Captain Barosa's voice boomed through the speakers on the console.

Darryl screamed. Emalynn shot Tristan a look to quiet the child.

"Saving your most valuable passenger. We'll be back just as soon as we can." She put a little more speed into their trajectory, keeping them hidden from the pirate ship while getting away.

"This isn't in your contract."

"Yes, it is." Emalynn worked to keep the shuttle moving and think of how to keep the captain from dragging her back. "It says I must do whatever is necessary to ensure the happiness and well-being of all passengers on the Pterodactyl. Trust me when I tell you I'm doing just that."

"Who is it?"

"It's best I don't tell you. But I promise he's that important."

She accelerated as fast as she could while staying in the Pterodactyl's shadow.

"Where are we going?" Tristan asked.

"I'm not sure yet."

#

"Git yer shit and git moving." Trace kicked Murphy awake. "We're closing on that girl you want. Don't know why yer so keen on her. You got yer choice right here."

Talli laughed too. Murphy had taken to sleeping fully clothed because of these two.

"Did we find her?" Murphy knew the question was stupid as soon as it was out.

"Poor innocent boy." Talli wrapped her arm around his shoulder. "You gonna have to find her yerself. Grab your bag and let's go. I don't wanna miss this raid. Should be rich."

Trace already had Murphy's bag and shoved it into his chest. "Captain says you leavin' us today. I still say you missed the best part of living here."

They dragged him through the halls of the ship. They had been redesigned to make moving around as confusing as possible. Murphy still couldn't go anywhere on his own without fear of getting lost. He hated the way it made him dependent on the pirates to get around. They never let him forget it either.

"You stay in the back and don't get in the way." Trace told him when they joined a dozen more pirates at an airlock. "Once we're on that ship, you ain't one of us anymore. Captain's orders. You do as yer told and we won't have to kill you."

Murphy nodded. This wasn't what he'd expected when he signed on, but he'd learned to expect it in his time here. He'd learned that whatever he'd thought when he joined them didn't hold enough water to feed a mouse. He just wanted to get this over with and be done with the pirates.

One of the women was working the controls by the airlock door. "Hah, got it. Ready to jump."

The women lined up, stunners in hand. They were also armed with just about everything except percussive weapons. Murphy just had his bag. He took his place at the end of the line. When the airlock opened, there wasn't much draft. Then the pirates were moving. They jumped feet first into the access tube. Murphy's stomach lurched as he left one gravity field and entered another. By the time he landed, they had the access port on the Pterodactyl open and were rushing in.

They took anything of value off anyone they passed and left them unable to follow. Some they stunned to unconsciousness; others were locked in closets or beaten over the head. This wasn't like the adventure vids. Murphy knew at any moment, he was going to become one of them in the eyes of the pirates.

A majority of the passengers were in the main ballroom of the luxury liner. They were dressed for the stars, glittering with precious stones and gold. The pirates took it all, separating the guests into groups.

"You. Get in there and keep yer head down." Trace grabbed Murphy by the shoulder and shoved him into a group of passengers. They were kind enough to break his fall.

He huddled with them even when the pirates left. No one was willing to risk being seen doing anything other than what they were told. Time dragged while they strained for some hint of what was happening.

When he was sure they were gone, he pushed himself off the floor.

"Are you trying to get us killed?" A woman pulled him back down.

"They're gone."

"How do you know?" another woman asked.

Murphy glared at her. She backed down and let him leave.

There was no one in the hall. He looked in both directions, but he still didn't know where to go. He took random turns until he found the crew area. The stark halls were easier to navigate, though he still didn't know what he was looking for. More random turns and trying of doors. He found the crew, bound together in a tangled pile.

He went back a few doors to a crew kitchen and grabbed as many knives as he could carry. It took a while to get the first woman free, but she was smart enough to distribute the knives to any hand that could use it. It didn't take long before someone took the knife from him and told him to go back to his cabin.

He faded into a corner until the room was almost cleared. A woman in a highly ornamented uniform came over to him.

"Thanks for helping out. What's your name?"

"Murphy."

"Nice to meet you, Murphy."

"Thanks. Um, what else can I do?"

"Just go back to your cabin now. We've got this."

He made himself as small as he could. "I don't have a cabin on this ship. They brought me with them."

The woman moved back just a bit. Murphy concentrated on not making eye contact.

"I see. Captain Barosa's going to want to talk to you." She

66

put a firm hand on his shoulder.

The bridge, when they got there, was still in a bit of chaos. The captain, with blood stains dripping down her cheek and a uniform more ripped than whole, stood in the middle, issuing orders to get the ship back up and running.

"Captain Barosa, this boy was left for us by those pirates."

The captain held up a hand, acknowledging them, but continued setting her ship in order. Murphy admired her strength as she led her crew. When she turned to him, that strength became intimidating.

"I've never heard of pirates leaving anything behind. What's your story?"

"I..." Murphy should have thought of a story before now. "I didn't know I was talking to a pirate when she offered to help me get here." He told her almost everything.

"Well, since you are the reason Emalynn decided to steal two of my passengers and a shuttle, you can work off the rest of her contract."

What contract?

CHAPTER EIGHT

EMALYNN – JUMPER SHUTTLE

Emalynn breathed a sigh of relief when she saw the shortwave connection to the Pterodactyl flicker and die. Just over two hours to get completely out of range. Their tablets were useless, both for them and anyone trying to track them. They were safe.

She released the straps holding her in her seat and floated toward the back.

"Where're you going?" Tristan looked alarmed.

"To the lav." She shook her head. The seat backs gave her convenient handholds along the way.

"But, we don't have gravity."

"Where would you put a gravity generator on a ship this size?"

She left him with that question and slid into the little stall. Despite having all the necessary gadgets, she came to agree with Tristan about gravity. The zero G made getting her jump suit back on even more of an adventure, including all the bumps and bruises to prove it.

When she rejoined the boys, Darryl was spinning and giggling right in the middle of the cabin.

"My turn," Tristan announced as he floated past her.

"I'm going to give us some gravity."

"I thought you said…"

"I'm going to spin the shuttle. Just brace yourself in there."

"I'll wait."

She floated up to grab Darryl and went to strap into the pilot's seat. Tristan took Darryl and strapped in next to her. Darryl fought to be with his Lyly this time. That only made the headache from the bumps in the lav worse. The thruster tanks were full, which gave her the idea. First, pick a direction. There was an Other corridor not far from here. She laid in the course first. Then, she used the thrusters to give the shuttle a spin. It wasn't much, but it let them stick to the floor at least.

"I'm not sure this is better." Tristan looked green. "My feet and head don't agree on down."

"Sorry." Her stomach was turning every which way. "When you can, try not to cross the center point."

She released her straps again and this time stayed in the chair. She dropped to the floor and the illusion of gravity took full effect.

Tristan followed her to the floor, with a sigh of relief. She moved out of his way to call Darryl down to the floor. The boy had found his way to the ceiling instead and was sitting there giggling at her. With a shake of her head, she jumped up and landed next to him. "Silly boy," she cooed as she scooped him into her arms.

"Mama," Darryl poked her in the nose. "Mama." He curled into her chest for a moment before pushing away to run around the ceiling. He was short enough to run under the tops of the seats. Emalynn let him run while she went to see what supplies they had. There were some emergency nutrition bars, enough for the fully loaded shuttle for one day, or for them, three weeks. They had about three days of oxygen in the tanks and filters enough to stretch another three. Water was going to be the issue. Even with the recycler running at full, it would only supply them for three days, four if they were conservative.

"What are you doing?" Tristan joined her at the supply closet.

"Noticing that we have enough fabric to recover all the seats at least twice and no diapers. We also don't have milk, or even nutrition powder. And to top that off, we have about three days of water."

Tristan sat back. "So we have to try to catch up to the Pterodactyl." He paled at that thought.

"No. That's not an option." She pulled the fabric out of the little cabinet. "Even if we could, it would be a death sentence for us to go back."

"Then what are we going to do?"

"Find water."

She laughed at the look of skepticism on his face.

"We're heading toward a known Other route. They eject water."

"It's not like they leave a river in space, either."

"No, but they are quite generous with their water and oxygen. That just leaves us with the problem of diapers." She pushed an armload of fabric into his hands, successfully breaking his thoughts about the Others. She dug out some scissors and they spent several hours cutting diapers from the fabric. They still had to send them through the sanitizer several times before they were soft enough to use.

The proximity alarm sounded while they were still cutting and folding.

"Others?" Tristan asked.

Emalynn had to get into the pilot's seat to see the read out. "Yup. We're in luck. It's a big one and moving slowly."

"What are you going to do? Just jump on their exhaust ports and hope they don't notice us?"

"Don't be silly. We could get killed doing that. I'm going to ask permission." She brought up the range of transmissions in use. It had been a long time since she'd seen anyone do this; she hoped she was remembering it right.

"How are you going to ask permission? Talking to the Others is impossible."

"Shh, I'm trying to remember."

"It's not something to remember. Communication has never been possible. No one has talked to the Others."

"No one has talked to Darryl yet." She looked up to where he'd fallen over to sleep. "It's not like I'm trying to negotiate a trade agreement. I just want to borrow their waste."

"You talk to the Others?"

"I wouldn't call it 'talking,' more like creative pantomime."

"When was this discovered?"

"I don't know. Some time before I was old enough to know what Baba was doing."

"There should have been an announcement."

"Right. Smugglers are going to announce how they get around the boarders and checkpoints." Emalynn shook her head.

The transmitters on the shuttle were weak, and the Other ship was moving slow. It would be a couple of hours before she could contact them with a secure enough link. That would give her time to work out what to do.

"Maybe you should put Darryl to bed somewhere more appropriate than the ceiling." Emalynn hid her flinch from the look he gave her. She needed to concentrate. She had to remember Baba, and that wasn't something she was willing to share yet.

#

TRISTAN - JUMPER SHUTTLE

Tristan finished tucking Darryl in for his nap in the back of the shuttle. They'd draped a curtain around some of the seats to make a separate room for him, but he still wasn't getting enough sleep. Tristan sighed as he crawled up the aisle. He was getting used to the odd gravity Emalynn had given them by spinning the shuttle, but he still couldn't walk straight when his head was on the opposite side of the rotation from his feet.

"It's time," Emalynn said when he reached the copilot's seat. "They are close enough for direct communication."

"You're sure about this?"

"As sure as I can be."

"But... aren't you afraid of starting a war?"

Emalynn laughed. "Is that what they tell you? Have you ever seen an Other for real?"

Tristan shook his head. He'd only see the pictures in documentaries. The first time had given him nightmares for weeks.

"I think they're pretty." Her fingers danced over the console and the screen filled with all kinds of strange colors. Slowly the image resolved itself into the weblike structures that defined the Others. They must have had eyes and mouths and hands, but Tristan had never been able to see where. Now that one was looking right at him, he found some eyes.

A stick floated into view and Emalynn raised her hand, keeping her fingers together and straight.

Then the image changed to an outline of their ship. Emalynn did something on the console and three red dots appeared in the outline. The dots turned blue. Emalynn pulled up a starscape with three systems highlighted in red. One of them turned blue.

"I guess we're going to the Devganni system," she said.

"What? What just happened?"

"I just asked for a lift. They're heading near Devganni so they'll take us there."

Tristan glanced over at his sister. "You talk to the Others?"

"Shh, don't tell anyone. It's a smuggler trick. Now quiet, I'm not done."

72

"But you said—"

"I still need to access their discharge ports. We don't have enough oxygen for the trip."

She turned back to the console and began typing again. The star map shrank to just the blue highlighted system and moved to the upper left corner of the screen. Then a blue outline of the Others' and a red outline of their shuttle appeared. Between them there were chemical diagrams of oxygen and water. Red lines moved from the Other ship to the Shuttle.

Emalynn leaned back to watch red arrows turn blue, followed by the outline of the shuttle. Then the shuttle moved just below the star chart. Finally, the Other ship outline grew and became more detailed. There were two small points highlighted in red. Emalynn leaned forward and pulled the shuttle back to the center and overlaid it on the red dots.

The Other held two sticks in vertical positions. Emalynn mimicked with her hands. Then the screen went blank.

"We've got our ride," Emalynn said. "Strap in. I'm going to have to land this thing and that means no gravity."

"Shit, I just got him to sleep," Tristan grumbled as he headed for the back of the shuttle.

"Hurry. They won't understand a delay."

Tristan pulled the sleeping boy onto his lap in one of the seats that made up his room and strapped in. As soon as the belt clicked, Emalynn canceled the rotation and Tristan felt his stomach lurch in the weightlessness. Darryl cried and pulled at the straps. It was all Tristan could do to keep the boy from hurting him. From back here, he couldn't see anything she was doing and it was all so slow he couldn't track the momentum changes either.

He did feel the first tugs of the artificial gravity as they approached the Other ship. He couldn't help but be relieved by the feel, even if he was sure they were about to start an interracial galactic war.

"Bump coming." Emalynn warned.

Tristan braced for it but barely felt it.

"You can unstrap now. We're on and locked."

Darryl squirmed out of Tristan's lap just as quick as he could and stumbled to Emalynn, who swooped him up in a big hug.

"Scary." Darryl buried his face in Emalynn's neck.

"Yeah, it was a little scary, wasn't it?" she cooed. "It's better now."

"Bet bet. Up up."

"Sorry, sweetie, that game won't work now."

Tristan could see a close-up of the Other ship at the bottom of the screen. It looked as weblike as the Others themselves. "How does that keep their atmosphere in?"

Emalynn shrugged. "It works for them."

Tristan stared at the ship they were sitting on for a moment longer. This was as close as anyone had ever gotten to the Others. Anyone official. "How did you learn to talk to them like that?"

"I wouldn't call that talking. It was mostly guesswork." Emalynn lifted Darryl up to touch the ceiling.

"Communication happened. How did you learn to do that?"

"I watched Baba." She let Darryl drop just a little to get him laughing.

"Do you realize what you've done?"

"I saved our butts."

"No... well, yes, but you also talked to the Others. This is a miracle."

She laughed. "Smugglers have been hitching on Others since before we were born. It's no miracle; it's survival."

#

MURPHY - PTERODACTYL

Murphy dropped the rag back into the cleaning solution, smiled at the security woman standing in the corner, and moved on to the next table. Captain Barosa had said that he would take on Emalynn's debt, not her contract. That debt now included the shuttle she and that Trevor kid had stolen. It chafed that he was stuck cleaning tables when he'd been so close. Worse was knowing it was his own fault. He couldn't call home. Davy wouldn't be able to get him out of this one. His parents would post him for losing her like this, and if she died, there'd be no chance of breathing their air. Until he could find another way off this luxury liner, he would clean everything they told him to clean.

"You're the boy who brought the pirates?" The stern voice made Murphy jump.

There was a man standing on the other side of the table he'd just washed. He had medium-dark skin with black, stick-straight hair and round, blue eyes. Those eyes looked like they could pierce his soul and pin it to the wall.

"Yes, sir." Murphy dropped the rag into his bucket and wiped his hands down the sides of his pants.

"And you knew Emalynn?"

Murphy could only nod. He thanked the stars that the table stood between them.

"Good." He walked away.

Murphy took a moment to breathe. The guard was still standing in the corner, only now she was smiling at him. Would she defend him if one of the passengers decided to take him? He didn't want to count on that. He went back to cleaning, losing himself in the rhythm of it.

There were forty-three tables in the dining hall. He was on table forty-two when the guard snapped to attention.

"Murphy." Captain Barosa strode across the room, swaying easily between the tables. Murphy didn't know if he should believe the cold set of her eyes or the slight upturn of her mouth.

"Yes, ma'am." He did his best impression of being at attention.

"This man just bought out your contract." The scary man from earlier stepped out from behind the captain. "You will do as he tells you. Understood?"

"Wait, you can't just sell me like that."

"I can and I did."

"What about my rights?"

"What rights? You don't exist on this ship."

Murphy bit back his next argument.

"You've got him." The captain turned to the man. "The shuttle will be ready in three hours. I hope you know what you're doing, sir."

"Thank you, Captain." He dipped his head toward her in respect.

Captain Barosa returned the gesture. She shot one more hate-filled look at Murphy, then left with the guard. This was crap. He wasn't a slave to be bought and sold.

"Calm yourself," the man said. "I promise not to have you cleaning tables."

Murphy only glared.

"If that's the way you like it, gather your things and meet me in the shuttle bay." He too left, with even more grace than the captain. At the door, he turned. "Before you think of doing anything else, I wouldn't like to see your chances with the captain if you fail. As she said, you don't exist right now."

Murphy put bucket and rag away before heading to the hole in the wall they called a room. He didn't need a lot of space, but a cell would have been roomier. Everything he had was packed. He'd only been on the Pterodactyl for a day. Still, he took the time to sit on the bed and stare at the room. *What just happened?*

In the shuttle bay, the man was already waiting for him, while some workers were crawling all over a shuttle. Murphy skirted the activity to join his new employer.

"Is that all?" The man eyed Murphy's small bag.

"Yeah."

"So the pirates weren't your first bad decision, then."

Murphy bit back another snide comment. The man stood perfectly still, while Murphy became more and more uncomfortable.

"We'll be working on your posture, then," the man said.

Murphy scowled and tried to stand still.

"We were never properly introduced. I'm Techani Kenchi."

"Murphy Sanchain."

"Good to meet you." The smile he wore was both genuine and disturbing.

"Why did you buy me?"

"I didn't. I bought your contract. There's a difference."

This man was annoying. "Fine, why did you buy my contract?"

"Because you have the most experience tracking Emalynn. And since she's with my nephew, I need your expertise."

Murphy swallowed hard. If he understood it right, this man had just bought him to track Emalynn. For once, the stars were lining up for him.

"How do you know they're together?" Murphy could kick himself for asking that question.

"Because she's the one he came here looking for."

The workers moved away from the shuttle and Mr. Kenchi reached down to pick up his own small bag. They stowed their belongings and strapped into the only two seats left in the shuttle—pilot and copilot. Murphy hoped Mr. Kenchi didn't expect him to do any actual navigating.

The shuttle bay doors opened and the shuttle floated out. It was just like on the vids. Murphy just sat back and enjoyed the scenery, until the thrusters kicked on, driving him back into his seat.

Murphy gripped the chair as though his life depended on it while they accelerated away from the big ship. When the force finally let up, Murphy turned to see Mr. Kenchi grinning at him.

"Do I have your attention?"

"You had it before."

"I needed all of your attention, not just the part that was looking for another reason to scowl at me. Tell me as much as you can about your girl."

CHAPTER NINE

MURPHY – LONG-RANGE SHUTTLE

Mr. Techani Kenchi's plan was simple. They returned to the exact coordinates where Emalynn and Trevor had left the Pterodactyl and then set a course matching their trajectory. All Murphy had to do was figure out how to track them in the vacuum between solar systems. Well, that and keep up with his studies and learn how to stand properly.

"If you stand properly, you will use less energy and make your body ready for anything," Techani had said. "Now find the stance again."

Murphy shook his body, then tried to make it back to the stance that Techani wanted. It should have been easy; it was just standing with his arms at his sides. Mr. Kenchi insisted on making it more complicated with bent knees and hips tucked in. He even made a fuss about how Murphy held his chest, shoulders, and chin.

"Very good." Techani offered a smile as a reward. "Now, do that ten more times and we'll start working on walking."

"Let me guess, walking isn't as natural as I think it is," Murphy said.

"It's as natural as standing. If you do it right, you will have more power."

Murphy sighed. What would Davy say if he were here? What a pit Murphy was becoming now. In debt up to his ears and taking orders from some old guy in a private shuttle. Yet there was nothing he could do about it. This old guy was his only shot at catching up with Emalynn.

He managed to attain a good enough stance three times before the alarm he'd set called them back to the console. They'd come to an Other trail. Murphy called up a detailed analysis of the chemical residue still dissipating.

"It's about a week old, maybe less." Murphy read out the report. "Eighty percent oxygen and... Oh, this is strange. Nineteen percent nitrogen. Others don't offgas nitrogen."

"Then we found where they changed course." Techani had pulled up his own analysis of the chemical trace.

"So which way did they go?"

Techani tapped at the console a bit. "Farther into the system."

Murphy looked at the readings on the system. "This is an Others colony. There's nothing here."

"The Others are here."

Why would Emalynn know anything about the Others or go to them? "There are rumors that smugglers use Other colonies to hide."

Techani glanced over at him. "Was Emalynn a smuggler?"

"No, but her mother was a mercenary."

Techani nodded and turned back to the console. "Strap in."

Murphy gripped the seat until their inertia stabilized again. Techani's hands were still hovering over the controls, so he didn't dare remove the restraints. Murphy pulled up a small window with the image from the forward sensors. How nice if they could just see the path. *The path,* he thought, *a path made of oxygen.* It took him a few tries to get the filter right, but then the Other trail was clear as day.

"Techani?"

"I'm concentrating."

"I have their path."

"I'm... What?"

Murphy transferred his image to the main screen.

"What is that?"

"I filtered to show only oxygen."

Those piercing blue eyes looked a bit warmer this time.

"I don't get it," Murphy said. "Why would they be following an Others' ship?"

Techani took a few deep breaths. "Perhaps to pick up the oxygen. It would extend their range, make it seem like they could make it in that little shuttle."

"But they'll still run out of power before they can get anywhere. What if we don't find them in time?"

Silence fell between them. Murphy looked out at the path before them. Somewhere along that way, the princess he'd been hunting most of his life was running scared. She went back to what she knew. "The other ways."

"Say that again."

Murphy hadn't noticed that he'd spoken.

"The other ways. It's what smugglers say when you ask them how they plan to evade detection. 'There are the other ways.' I guess it makes sense now." Murphy waved at the path on the screen.

"What do you know of smugglers?" Techani turned his seat to face Murphy head on.

Murphy couldn't look away from the intensity in his eyes. "Um, I just heard some things..." The intensity grew. "My parents... they weren't smugglers, but sometimes they used them. I listened in." There was no relief from that stare. "Mother always complained that they insisted on using small shuttles rather than cargo ships and the women would just laugh and say cargo ships were too easy to spot. So Mother wanted to know how they were going to avoid detection with a short-range shuttle out between the stars. They'd laugh again and say 'the other ways.'"

Techani looked away. Murphy took a deep breath, thankful to be out from under that stare.

"Perhaps they were saying the Others' ways. A short-range shuttle still wouldn't be able to make the crossing between the stars, even gathering the oxygen here." Techani brought his stare back to Murphy. "What would your Emalynn know about this?"

"I don't kn—" He flinched under that stare. "She talked about smuggling with her mother, but it didn't make much sense. She was crying that night and I never got another chance to ask her."

"Her mother?"

"A mercenary who kidnapped her as a baby, then ended up raising her, but Baba was ungraduated. She would have had to take whatever jobs paid. Emalynn traveled a lot as a child, perhaps with the smugglers."

"You think she would smuggle herself? She's in a short-range shuttle and paranoid."

Murphy nodded.

#

81

"Are you up for learning to be a farmer?" Emalynn asked.

"What?" Tristan was in the back of the shuttle, practicing his forms.

"In the next system there are two colonies. One is a bustling hub with all the luxuries, a royal outpost, and people who will probably recognize you on every corner. The other is primitive, still lacking in basic net gear, and has only one town. There may be one or two of the original colonists still alive. Most of the people won't care enough about the monarchy to know that you're supposed to be dead."

Tristan gave her a face. "We don't have any other options?"

"Not in that system, and we don't have enough food to make it to the next. I vote for the primitive. They will welcome us as long as we are willing to work. It's the best place to hide, really. Who's going to think of looking for the prince in a corn field?"

"I guess." He started his form again.

Emalynn watched him for a moment, then turned her attention to Darryl, who was playing in the copilot's seat. It took a while for her to recognize that he was playing at being her.

"Go da." He pointed to the main screen, then poked at the inert controls.

"Yeah, we'll go there." She pulled up the star map to show the route to Farthing Moon. "Six days."

Tristan harrumphed.

"You don't like the idea."

"Not really. I want to go home."

"Home? Where they're trying to kill you?"

"You don't have to point that out." He harrumphed again.

"I want to go home too." At least he had a home to dream about.

"Sorry, I'm being a whiny bitch."

Emalynn flinched. "You have good reason to be whiny."

"So do you, but..."

"Whining never gets you anywhere so why bother?" She shrugged. "That doesn't make the reason go away."

Something beeped. The console showed only the charts she'd put up for Darryl. She looked at Tristan, who was as wide eyed as she was. The beep came again from somewhere mid-cabin.

"Col wer." Darryl bounced out of the chair and ran to his simple tablet.

The tablets were useless without net access, and they didn't have a transmitter on this shuttle. Emalynn shifted to be out of sight from the camera on her tablet just in time for its screen to light up.

"Ly, don't panic." Murphy appeared on screen next to Master Kenchi. "We are coming. We haven't told anyone else where we are or where you are. Ly, just let us know you got this."

He sounded almost desperate. She was about to ask Tristan about it when his tablet came to life with the same image. This time it was the man who spoke.

"Trevor, you are in danger. There is no telling what the Others will do if they catch you on their ship. We are not far behind you. If you drop off the ship, we will be able to find you."

The tablet died again.

"Col wer?" Darryl complained.

Emalynn grabbed her tablet and pulled the battery. Tristan was only seconds behind her. They dropped the tablets back into the seats.

"Who was that?" Tristan asked.

"His name is Murphy." Emalynn glanced at the tablets now facedown on the seat. "He was my boyfriend, kind of. He's supposed to be back at school, making up for my absence in our group project."

"What are they doing here?"

"Following us." Emalynn went back to the pilot's seat. "But how? And can we believe them?"

"Why wouldn't we?" Tristan grabbed Darryl's tablet before he smashed it into the floor again. "We know them."

He was right, but something was wrong. "How did they find each other?"

He opened his mouth but closed it again without saying anything. His eyes were flashing back and forth as he came to the conclusion that there might be someone else involved.

"I don't know how Murphy even got off planet. He used up his savings for me. I can't trust him now, not until I figure it out."

Tristan nodded. "So what do we do?"

"I don't know. Until I know how they're tracking us..." She could only shrug.

Tristan turned to comfort Darryl, who was still trying to get his "col wer" game back. Emalynn turned toward the pilot's seat, where the star charts might offer some clues.

"Is it possible they were just broadcasting?" Tristan asked. "I mean, do we even know if they're tracking us?"

"No, they knew about the Others' ship… They knew about the Others. They aren't tracking us; they're tracking the Others." Emalynn reconfigured the shuttles aft sensors and was able to see the bright trail of oxygen that defined an Other trail.

"We can't silence that."

"No, but we can use it to our advantage." Emalynn pulled up the navigation simulator and started entering the parameters.

"What do you mean?" Tristan came over to watch her.

She held up her hand for a moment to stall his questions. If she were right, it would be possible to mask their deviation. All she had to do was figure out how.

"Look at the oxygen trail." She put the aft sensors back on the screen. "See how wide it gets."

Tristan nodded.

"We've recharged the thrusters with oxygen, not nitrogen." She pulled up the specs on the thrusters. "Not enough, I'll have to purge them."

"Why oxygen?"

"'Cuz the Others give off more than we need for life support. And they don't give up nitrogen. But if I can make all the course corrections with oxygen, they'll be hidden in the Others' trail."

"That's going to be tricky." Tristan poked at the copilot controls and grumbled when they were still blocked.

Emalynn laughed and toggled them back on. "True, but we have a couple of days to figure it out." She opened a second copy of the navigation simulator with her specs and sent it to his side of the screen.

"We're going to the primitive colony." It was a statement, not a question.

"It's all we've got right now."

#

TRISTAN - JUMPER SHUTTLE

Tristan tried to follow Emalynn's frantic calculations. Even though they'd taken the batteries out of the tablets, he couldn't shake the feeling they were still being tracked. Emalynn looked for a way to change their course, to shake their followers. Tristan, never all that skilled at navigation, couldn't see half of what she did. He tried to ask her to explain, but she just snapped at him that this was difficult and to just leave her alone.

Darryl cried when she barked. He wanted to play with her, but she didn't have time for that either. Every waking moment she studied the charts and made calculations. Tristan had to swallow his own frustration to keep Darryl away from Emalynn. By the third day of this, he'd lost his patience too.

"I got it." Emalynn startled him while he was changing Darryl's diaper.

"Damn it."

"If we break here, rather than waiting to get closer, we can save more of our momentum and only have to do a minor course correction that will be completely hidden in the trail from the Others' ship."

He finished changing Darryl and washed the mess off his hands before coming over to look. She had a lot of navigational calculations on the screen that he couldn't read. "What did you find? Can we do that?"

"We're fully charged now. We can last for six days."

Tristan nodded and pulled Darryl into his lap in the copilot's seat. "Should we strap in?"

"Probably."

There wasn't much to watch other than the Other ship falling away. The course correction was as tiny as she'd said. She'd added the rotation that gave them a sense of down.

"I'm going to miss gravity." Tristan moaned.

"Just five days and then we'll land on Farthing Moon."

"I thought we were going into orbit?"

She bit her lips a little. "Actually, we're going to crash."

"What?"

"It will make our sob story of being caught in a pirate attack a bit more believable." Emalynn unstrapped and climbed to her place on the ceiling of the shuttle. "And we can go back to Darryl's favorite game."

Tristan sighed. It was true. He released the straps and pushed Darryl toward Emalynn. He slipped into his place on the floor just in time to catch Darryl.

"Is there any way to test if we were successful?" Tristan asked. Darryl was his usual giggly self again for the moment. Tristan pushed him back across to Emalynn.

She caught him in a big hug that he had to struggle out of. "I don't know." She pushed Darryl back. "I kept all the discharges in the trail of the Others' ship, but I don't know how we're being tracked."

"So we're running quiet now?"

"I've only got the life support systems and proximity sensors running."

They passed Darryl a couple times in silence.

"Tell me about our father. He has to be a real person under all that propaganda."

Tristan let her pull him into the conversation. He didn't have a lot to tell her about Father, or Mother, but took what he could about life in the palace. Compared to the life she'd led, it sounded too glamorous for how it felt to him. Her adventures with Baba were much more interesting to him.

They were still working on the story they would tell the colonists when they arrived at Farthing Moon. Emalynn fell into the pilot's seat. Darryl followed her, climbing into her lap. Tristan got into the copilot's seat.

"We're going to have to be weightless for a while." Emalynn passed Darryl over, unwinding his fingers from her hair with practiced ease.

"Gee, thanks." Tristan caught him up and strapped into their seat. "We're going to be landing soon. You need to sit with Daddy so Mama can keep us safe."

"Daddy." He squealed.

"This is going to get rough." Emalynn warned him just before she stopped the rotation.

"Are you sure about this?"

"As sure as I can be." Her fingers flowed over the controls again. Tristan took a deep breath to keep Darryl from noticing how scared he was.

"We've made orbit," Emalynn announced.

The shuttle lurched and shook. Darryl giggled.

"Shuttle, you are in unstable orbit." A voice came from the console.

"I don't know what to do!" Emalynn sounded a lot more scared than she looked.

"You need to stabilize your pitch. You are descending."

"I can't. We're out of rear thrust."

"Holy crap."

"We're going to crash?"

Tristan could hear, but not see, the tears streaming down her cheeks.

"No, just do exactly as I say and you'll land safely. Our emergency crews are already ready."

"I'll try."

"What controls do you have?"

"The front thrusters are still charged and I have more in the right... I mean, starboard thrusters."

"What about life support?"

"Umm..." She paused long enough to smile at Tristan. "It says twenty-five percent."

"That's good." The voice was relieved. "You're going to route some of your oxygen into the rear thrusters."

"What? No, we need that to breathe."

Tristan tried not to laugh at her acting. She was brilliant.

"We aren't going to route all of it. Here's what you need to do..." The woman on the other end started giving directions that Tristan couldn't follow. Emalynn made it sound like she didn't quite know what she was doing. All the while, the shuttle was lurching about, getting lower in the orbit.

"Now you can stabilize," the woman said.

"It's still not working." Emalynn complained.

"Calm down, it's going to be subtle. Do you have an autopilot?"

"No, I can't find one. I tried. Don't you have remote?"

"We're still a starter colony. We don't have that kind of tech yet."

"What am I going to do?" Emalynn cut the connection. "Hold on tight. We're about to set down and I need to make a crash trail."

Darryl's giggles had turned to tears. The shuttle started bouncing against the tops of trees. Tristan couldn't keep his eyes open as they dropped below the top of the canopy. Then with a couple big lurches, they stopped.

"Is everyone okay?" Emalynn asked.

She held her shoulder, but blood dripped from a gash on her forehead.

CHAPTER TEN

MURPHY – LONG-RANGE SHUTTLE

Murphy sat in the navigator's seat, watching the readouts on the oxygen trail they were following. It was the most boring thing he could think of, but it was this or have Techani come up with something he should be practicing. The trail hadn't changed since they'd picked it up. The Others were traveling at a constant speed in a straight line between stars. The detectable oxygen spread in a predictable pattern.

One of the numbers was out of line. At the far edge of their sensor range, there was a spike in the in the oxygen. He zoomed in to be sure. The trail spiked to the right as well, then just died.

"I think they left the Others there." Murphy highlighted the place where he'd seen the spike.

Techani leaned forward to look at the data. "I don't see a trail branching from there."

"It's small." Murphy zoomed even closer, highlighting the slight bulge he'd seen.

"What makes you think that's where they left?"

"The trail has been amazingly consistent up to here. This is the only deviation."

Techani nodded. He pulled up the star charts. Murphy saw his objection even before he said it. "Where would they go from here?"

Murphy overlaid the oxygen trail on the star chart. New data broadened the spike just a bit and gave him something to calculate a vector. Emalynn was paranoid. That had to be important here. That and the vector was barely ten degrees off from their former course. He traced it through the star charts and found an inhabited system just four days out.

"There."

Techani had been watching him work and nodded with respect. "That would take a lot of skill."

"Which Emalynn has. Captain Barosa said she'd beat the junior simulation record by two days."

Techani shot him a piercing look.

"That's what she said, honest."

"So you think she would actually be able to do it?"

"I'm saying she might try. I'm also saying that I think she might be paranoid enough to try to hide their tracks in a maneuver like that. Would Trevor try to talk her out of it?"

"He's probably pretty paranoid too."

Techani laid in the new course. Murphy stifled his joy at having shown the old man that he had some skills. Techani would make the training session harder. At least he was getting some good exercise in the low gravity. And plenty of study time. They were able to set up alarms to detect changes in the background chemical signature.

As they approached the system, the alarms became useless. Too much traffic made it impossible to detect a single shuttle's thrusters. More so if you assumed that the shuttle would use as little thrust as possible to avoid detection. The system had two colonies, one established and the other still primitive.

"What do you know about her?" Techani asked. "Where would she go?"

The two colonies couldn't be more different, but each of them had benefits for the paranoid looking to stay hidden. The planet colony was close to maximum population. The Moon didn't have a fulltime net connection. Which one would Emalynn choose? Would Trevor change that calculation?

"I'd guess the small one. It's got less tech there."

"You don't think someone with the skills you claim wouldn't go where her skills would work best?"

Murphy hadn't thought about it that way. She did know how to avoid the cameras. What else had Baba taught her?

"I suppose." Murphy admitted.

"And that's where they are going to have the most options to move on from."

Techani laid in a course for the older colony. Murphy wasn't so sure of the logic. What if she was going for a long-term place to hide?

#

Tristan did his best to bandage Emalynn's head while Darryl clung to her. There was a fire starter kit in the emergency supplies, but the directions were anything but clear. He tried until it got too dark to see what he was doing. They ended up huddling under the emergency blankets in the shuttle to keep warm until morning.

"Is everyone all right?"

Tristan woke to the call.

"We're here." Tristan pulled himself out of the pile. "We're here." He walked stiffly to the open back door. He'd tried to close it last night, but with the power gone, he didn't have the strength to do it.

A team of medics, three men and a woman, were climbing out of a huge transport. The wheels, wrapped in a track, were taller than he was. The medics were all business. One coming to check out Tristan while the others took on Darryl and Emalynn.

"Mama Ly." Darryl clung to Emalynn even as the medics tried to assess him for injuries.

"Sweetie, come here." Tristan pulled Darryl off, but his weight was more than he could hold. The medics were there to help hold him up and catch Darryl.

The woman started asking Tristan questions about why the three of them were flying alone in the shuttle.

"Pirates." Tristan found it hard to concentrate on the story they'd decided on. "Pirates mad that we didn't have anything to give them."

"What pirates?"

"On the ship. Umm... Pterodactyl. They attacked and when we couldn't give them anything, they pushed us into the shuttle. Is she okay?"

They were putting Emalynn on a stretcher.

"Just a precaution."

"Lynn." Tristan tried to follow, but his own weakness stopped him.

"Hold it there." The woman caught him before he fell off the edge of the shuttle. "You're going to need help too." She waved one of the medics over. "Check his muscle density."

The man nodded and pulled out a clamp like tool. "This won't hurt." He pinched Tristan's upper arm. "Twenty-three percent," he read off the scanner.

Darryl was still screaming to bring down the moon.

"What's going on?"

"Those diapers, what were you thinking?" the man asked, putting away his clamp.

"It's what we had."

Looks were passed around the team. They gave him a pill and made him drink far more water than he wanted. Before long, he was leaning against the side of the shuttle, just watching them move about the wreck, taking vid of the whole scene, including his failed attempt at a fire. When they came to put him on a stretcher, he couldn't object.

Tristan woke on a soft bed with a heavy blanket draped over him. He rolled over to find Emalynn in bed with him, still pale and breathing shallowly, her head bound in fabric bandages. He wanted to touch them but thought better of that.

They were in a small, rough wood hut. Light came from around the shuttered windows and the low fire burning in the stone fireplace. Darryl was sleeping in a polished wood crib next to his side of the bed.

Just sitting up made him breathe hard. He sat on the edge of the bed until he caught his breath. He made it to the little bench beside the door, where his shoes were waiting for him. He regained his breath again, then lost it putting his shoes on. He should have known this was a problem. They'd been in minor gravity for so long. He would just have to work at regaining his strength.

The door opened to a world bathed in cool blue light. He clung to the doorframe for a moment. Where could he go from here? All he could see were little huts that all looked the same.

"Good, you're awake," said the man sitting just outside the door. "We were a little worried. How long were you living on those nutrition bars?"

"About three weeks."

"Yeah, they aren't really meant for long-term use," the man said. "How are you feeling now?"

"Fine, I guess. A little hungry." Unless they were going to give him more nutrition bars.

"Let me show you to the cookhouse. It's a bit late for dinner and too early for breakfast, but there's always soup." He held out his arm for Tristan to cling to.

Tristan hated to admit he needed the help, but just standing up, even holding on to the door, was difficult. They barely made it to the corner of the hut before he was breathing heavily. The man, Neil, slowed to a pace Tristan could maintain.

The cookhouse was a larger hut filled with rough wood tables. Each table had a candle in the middle, though most of them weren't lit. Neil brought Tristan to the first table inside the door and lit the candle. Tristan sank into a chair with arms and a back, though most of the tables were surrounded with benches.

"I'll get you some soup." Neil left him there.

Everything about this place screamed "locally made." From the wood tables, polished only on the tops, to the worn wood floors. On Prime, wood was a luxury used sparingly to highlight a design. Here, it showed a level of poverty. Even the bowl and cup Neil brought back were made of wood. The spoon, though, was a simple steel, a relief to Tristan.

"Here, take this first." The man handed him a small pill.

"What is it?"

"Muscle builder. It will help you get used to the gravity."

"Aren't these illegal?"

"Only in professional sports. And they will only hurt you if you take more than you need. Most people will be fine with one, so that's all you'll get around here."

Tristan pushed his doubts aside and swallowed the pill. The soup was an amazing blend of flavors. The only reason he took his time was that the spoon was so heavy.

#

EMALYNN - FARTHING MOON

Emalynn woke with a headache and the sense that she needed to do something. She was lying on something soft, but it was still hard to breathe under the weight of the blanket covering her. She opened her eyes to see wood rafters over her, with light coming from somewhere, just enough for her to make out the rough beams. They were in the village, thank the stars.

"Ma, ma, ma, ma," Darryl called from her right.

She turned her head to look at him, but everything went swirly. She had to close her eyes again.

"Ma, ma, ma, ma." Darryl became more insistent.

"Sorry, darling. I'm right here."

"MA!"

She cracked her eyes open. Darryl was standing in a wood crib. The wood was polished to shine.

"Oh, sweetie. I'm coming."

Sitting up was impossible. Any movement took every straight line and bent it into curves. The more she tried, the more she felt her stomach was going to crawl up her throat and run away.

"MAAAAAAAAAAAAAAAAAAAAAAAAAAA!"

His scream brought shining splotches of color into her vision.

"What's all the screaming about?" asked a strange voice asked. "Oh now, little one, you need to let your mama sleep."

A slender man came into view. He looked vaguely familiar. "Who...?"

"Oh, you're awake." He turned, still holding Darryl over his shoulder. Darryl struggled to get to her. "How are you feeling?"

"Like crap. What happened?" She tried not to move while she spoke but had to keep her eyes closed anyway.

"You hit your head in the crash. From the looks of it, you were lucky that was all that happened."

"Mamamamamamamama." Darryl leaned toward her.

Emalynn held out her arms. The man put Darryl on her other side. The movement of the bed was more than she could take with her eyes open. Darryl put his head on her stomach, cooing at her.

"Who are you?" Emalynn asked when she could open her eyes again.

"Oh, sorry... I'm Neil."

"Thank you. I'm Lynn."

"Welcome to Farthing Moon, I guess. Not the best welcome, but I'm sure you'd rather wait for the party."

Emalynn smiled. "Thank you. Can you tell me about this colony?"

"Oh, I thought... Of course. Farthing Moon was colonized only about forty years ago. We're still working out the calendar to match Galactic norm." He shrugged. He confirmed that the colony didn't have much tech and didn't trust what they did have. Their contract gave them seventy-five years to begin paying the debts of creating the colony, so they were still just subsistence now. "The less the company knows about what we're doing the better. I hope to never meet a company rep."

Emalynn smiled. This was perfect, even more than she had hoped. A primitive colony wouldn't even have checked their IDs yet.

"Where is Trevor?" she asked.

"He went to the cookhouse. Are you hungry?"

She hadn't been until he mentioned it.

"Well, you can nurse him while I get you something to eat." Neil got up to leave.

"He's formula fed." This could tear a life-sized hole in their story.

Neil stopped on his way out the door. "But there were no bottles…"

"We softened the nutrition bars for him." No need to lie there. Darryl had hated it as much as they had, but it kept them all full.

"That's no good. I'll get something for him too. You try to sleep."

Emalynn hated taking orders like that. Her body, however, was at its limit and she couldn't even find the strength to argue.

CHAPTER ELEVEN

TRISTAN – FARTHING MOON

The first day was an epic struggle between boredom and exhaustion. Tristan's mind was ready to take on the new life, but his body was still fighting the gravity. The colonists pretty much left him alone as he stumbled about the town, except the medics who stopped to check his vital signs every time they saw him and offer him encouragement to keep going. The second morning, he made it to breakfast on his own, which was all they needed to see.

"Looks like you're ready, then." A gruff looking woman sat down opposite him with her own plate of eggs and sausage.

Tristan had chosen the oatmeal with mixed fruit, most of which he couldn't identify. Eggs were a mixed blessing as far as he was concerned, since you could never really tell where they came from. His stomach tried to run away when he looked at the greasy sausage.

"Ready for what?" He forced himself to put the spoonful of oatmeal in his mouth.

"Smart boy. Ready to start earning your keep." She spoke around the bite of eggs she'd taken. "What skills have you got?"

"Umm…" He didn't have any. Well, none that applied to life on a primitive colony. "I don't know. I wasn't in the colonization track."

"'Colonization track…' Would you listen to the boy?" A man with a plate loaded with just about everything sat next to the woman. "Rose, what are you going to do with this kid?"

"Teach him to kick you in the teeth." She pushed his plate down a couple of seats. "Don't mind Roger. He's just jealous 'cause you look cuter than him."

Roger could have been a model if his skin wasn't so

suntanned. His hair, neatly braided down his back, was that enviable shade just a little lighter than black. Tristan could have been jealous of his beauty if he cared about such things.

"Well, we're going to have to find something for you to do. You ever work with animals?"

"No."

"You ever live on a planet before?"

"Yeah, but only in the cities."

"Oh, a city boy," Roger put it.

"Would you shut it?" Rose glared at Roger. "You want to try?"

"You gonna throw him in with the cows?" Roger laughed. "Teach those slim hands how to massage a teat? That'll be worth watching."

"One more word and you're teaching him how to milk a cow."

Roger stopped laughing.

Tristan couldn't even imagine what they were talking about. He'd seen pictures of cows and knew some kinds of milk came from them, but the rest made no sense to him. Yet another major gap in his knowledge. For now, he just filled his mouth with oatmeal and tried not to look at Roger.

"I'm thinking you'd do better with the sheep anyway."

Tristan swallowed hard. "I'm going to milk sheep?"

Everyone for several tables around burst out laughing at that. Tristan's cheek burned with embarrassment. People farther away wanted to know what was so funny. Tristan heard several stumbling attempts to explain what he'd said, with new outbursts of laughter after each one. How he wished he could just crawl through a crack in the floor.

"Oh, honey, you really are a city kid, aren't you? Some corporate bust or something, am I right?" Rose wiped tears from her eyes.

"Something like that." Tristan admitted.

"Well, life's a bit different here." She smiled at him in a motherly sort of way. "We don't put much stock in fashion, for one thing, and we're all equal here. Don't go imposing your corporate structures on us, hear?"

Tristan shook his head.

"Now finish that bowl of oats. You're going to need it."

After breakfast, Tristan followed Rose out of town to the north. The animal barns were there, she explained, because the

98

wind here rarely came from the north. Even in a starter colony, they didn't want to live with the smells of animals wafting over the town. As they got closer, Tristan came to understand why. The smell was gag-inducing, though Rose promised he would get used to it before long.

The barns were long structures, about twice the height of anything in town. Rose named them as they went past. This one for horses, then the milk cows, followed by the beef cows. He didn't ask about the difference. There were turkeys and chickens in separate coops. She didn't know why they called the same structure something different just because there were birds living there, but they did. Next came the llamas, goats, and sheep and just over the last little hill, she pointed to the pigs and hogs. Again, she couldn't tell him the difference, but then she'd never really cared for language.

"It's more important that you know how to treat the animals than to know what they're called, unless you're trying to sell 'em, which I stay out of." She slid open the door on the end of the sheep barn and waved Tristan in ahead of her. "Like I said, we'll start you with the sheep. They aren't smart enough to figure out you're a city boy. As long as you give them food, they'll like you just fine and won't try anything goofy."

"What do you mean?"

"Well, take goats. They're crafty critters and like to get out of the fence. Not so bad around here—we keep the wild predators under control near the colony—but they can get lost, and we really can't afford to lose any. So if they were to trick you, which they will, it'll take a lot of work to get them rounded back up. The sheep, they don't seem to notice there's a bigger world out there. So you can learn what to do without having to worry if they're going to get one over on ya."

Tristan nodded as though that all made sense. He hoped once he saw the animals it would. In the meantime, all he had to do was focus on what she told him to do and the rest would come with time.

"Hey, Mav," Rose called into the dark building. "Mav, get out here."

There were a lot of sounds that Tristan couldn't identify. *Must be from all the sheep they have.* Thankfully, his nose had gone on strike and quit telling him about the scents.

A slender woman with a leathery appearance appeared halfway down the center aisle of the barn. "What now? I got a ewe giving birth here."

"And I've got an apprentice for you."

"By the stars." The woman moved back to where she was. "I hope she has a strong stomach."

"It's not that bad." Rose led Tristan down the aisle. "He'll have to learn sometime."

Mav looked back at them. "He?"

"Don't tell me you have a problem with that." Rose winked at Tristan. "Trevor's going to need the basics. He was corporate before he crashed here."

They'd reached the place where Mav was standing, arms crossed over her chest. She gave Tristan a quick up and down look. "Well, he looks healthy enough. Why me?"

"'Cuz you're the best we got." Rose patted Tristan on the back. "Shoulda seen him pushing through the gravity yesterday. Kid doesn't give up easy. We need more of that 'round here."

"What are you talking about?" Mav shifted her gaze to Rose. "We all do all we can."

"There just aren't quite enough of us."

"There will be."

"But he's here now."

Tristan felt a little odd just standing there. "What about the sheep?" He tried to look innocent.

Mav shot one more look at Rose. "Right, kid. Hell, you aren't even dressed right. Up there's a cabinet. Find something to cover those clothes. We'll get you real clothes later. Don't forget a pair of gloves. Then get back here."

Rose was already gone. Tristan went to find the cover-ups. It was a bit thrilling to think he was about to learn something real. By the time he returned to the little hut with Emalynn, he was exhausted and happier than he'd ever been.

"This is going to be fun." He flopped on the bed beside her.

"You smell like a failed recycle system." She pushed him away.

"I smell like sheep."

"If you say so. Go wash up." She smiled at him.

#

MURPHY – RISEN COLONY

Murphy could find no trace of Emalynn, Trevor, or Darryl. While Techani met with contacts, with equally bad results, Murphy had been hacking into every system he could find. He checked every system with an ID reader from security doors to transit systems. Techani kept them moving at the oddest hours, proving that someone could be more paranoid than Ly.

"I think we made a mistake," Murphy said as soon as Techani came back from wherever he'd been.

"What kind of mistake?"

"They aren't here."

"You were so sure they were." Techani came to look over Murphy's shoulder. "How did you change your mind?"

Murphy fidgeted with the edge of his tablet. "Evidence would suggest that I was wrong and history will back it up."

Techani settled on the only other chair in the small room they were renting for today and pulled out his own tablet. Murphy watched him for a moment, then turned back to his data. They would be moving again soon. Techani never came back to a place more than three times, and this was his third time walking through that door.

"If they aren't here, where do you think they are?" Techani didn't even look up from his tablet.

Murphy shrugged. "Maybe they weren't on the Other ship. Or they didn't get off where we thought they did."

"Do you believe either of those?"

Honestly? Could he honestly believe anything at this point? "No, but they aren't here. So where could they be?"

"On the primitive colony." Techani flipped his tablet around for Murphy to see.

There was a grainy image of a crashed shuttle among unmanaged trees. There wasn't enough detail in the image to identify the shuttle or even how long it had been there.

"What is that?" Murphy grabbed the tablet to get a better look.

"I'm not sure. It was taken by our shuttle on the way past the moon. Have you found anything about a crash in the colony reports?"

Colony reports? He hadn't even thought to look at the reports for Farthing Moon. "Not yet."

"Get on it."

The door slid open, filling the room with soldiers in full armor. Two of them yanked Murphy off his chair, pinning his arms behind him. Three others were between him and Techani.

"You are advised to remain silent. You are being recorded for later prosecution."

"What?" Murphy asked.

"Tell only the truth," Techani called over the noise of the soldiers.

They were dragged out to an armored but unmarked transport. Murphy tried to walk for himself, but the soldiers kicked his legs out from under him.

"Bastards." Murphy growled.

A soldier pulled him up by his hair. "You are to keep quiet until we ask you questions."

They threw him in the back of the transport—an empty box without even benches to sit on. Murphy struggled to sit up and move out of the way before they tossed Techani in with him. When Techani landed on the floor of the transport, he was unconscious and covered in blood.

The ride to jail was jarring. This transport didn't obey the governed speeds required in the city or slow down sensibly before taking a turn. By the time they arrived, Murphy was as bloody as Techani and almost as unconscious. He had just enough wits about him as the soldiers pulled him from the truck to know they weren't at a standard law station. He'd be willing to bet they weren't in a city. He was sure they wouldn't be recorded anywhere either.

Dear stars, what have I gotten into now?

#

EMALYNN – FARTHING MOON

Emalynn stood with Tristan in front of the colony council. They'd lived here for weeks, using colony resources and giving very little back. Tristan had begun to learn farming, but he had a long way to go. Physical labor hadn't been part of his upbringing. Emalynn was still recovering from the crash and building up her stamina. It was a struggle just to keep standing.

They'd spun a tale of forbidden love, ripped from the vids of corporate families. Their families were rivals and forbade the love between the two impulsive young students. They sort of glossed over how they ended up with Darryl. Now all they wanted was a place where they could be who they wanted to be without anyone worrying about the business implications.

"We've looked into your IDs." Mav spoke first. Emalynn could see the doubt in her eyes "There are many inconsistencies."

Emalynn took a deep breath and dropped her eyes to the floor. "I had them hacked. We wouldn't have gotten off station with our real IDs."

"How can you know that you will want to live on a primitive colony?" Charra, David's mother, asked.

"I know we're taking a risk." Emalynn looked to Tristan but continued before he could take up the story. "But I think we'll make it. All the tech we used to have didn't help us be happy. It tied us to families that cared more about our image than us."

"How do you know this is what he wants?" Charra countered.

"We don't." Tristan squeezed Emalynn's hand. "How could we? But we know what it would be like to grow up in the rivalry, and no kid deserves that." There was more truth to this part of the story than Emalynn knew.

"Enough." Griffen called everyone's attention. "The question before the council is: will we welcome these two young people into our lives? They have asked for our protection, and to give that, we will have to falsify our reports for years to come. They have proven themselves willing to learn our ways and give what they can to the community. How say you?"

Mav spoke first. "They aren't the first to ask for our protection and they won't be the last. They are better suited to this way of life than the last refugees we took in. I vote yes."

"We're not voting yet." Griffen shook his head. "Next?"

"It is a risk in more than one way." A woman Emalynn hadn't met yet spoke. She hadn't looked at them through the whole meeting. "There's the obvious: their families, the lord, or our backer—do we know their relationship with DiaCo? We also risk that their willingness does not translate into ability."

Charra spoke next. "We all risk here. We don't have the tech to recover from accidents the way some colonies do. I say if they're willing, that's enough for me."

No one else chose to speak. The vote came out unanimous in their favor. Emalynn let out a sigh as she sat down. Tristan sat with her.

"We did it."

She nodded. "Now the question is: what did we do?"

"We changed our lives."

That they had, but was it really a change she could live with? So many questions that hadn't mattered before beat against the inside of her head. What about Darryl's family? What about her own? She had lived this long without knowing them, but now she knew. They'd just won the fight that would keep her from them for the rest of her life as well.

"Oh, honey, it's been a hard time, hasn't it?" Charra held her shoulders.

Emalynn could only nod.

She cried on shoulder after shoulder until she was back with Charra. "It's time for you to get home, dearie." The woman lifted Emalynn with ease and carried her to the little hut that had become theirs.

"What's going on?" Tristan asked when they were safely behind the closed door.

"I don't know?"

He held her shoulders. "What are you feeling so guilty about?"

He knew. Just like he'd told her. She could feel his confusion too. Words weren't enough, but they were all she had. She cried them into his shoulder. She told him all her doubts and fears. How she'd hoped to make Baba proud.

"And now, what have we just done?"

"What do you mean?"

"We've just kidnapped ourselves again. We aren't going back."

"We aren't going back." Tristan's voice held none of the pain and sorrow she felt. "We've made our choice and this is it."

"How can you just give it up like that?"

"If I hadn't been a brat that day, I still wouldn't be prince. I just wanted a little freedom, and I got this. Let one of our cousins take on the challenge."

"But I thought... Everyone wants to be royal."

He pulled himself away. "Everyone doesn't understand. I've lived that life, and I get a chance to choose. I choose you. I choose here. I choose. You don't know how wonderful that is."

CHAPTER TWELVE

MURPHY - THE DUNGEON

Murphy lay on the floor of the cell where his tormentors had dropped him. He'd lost track of the number of times they'd dragged him from the dark into the bright interrogation room to ask him the same stupid questions over and over. He'd lost interest in the questions, or in what they wanted him to say. He didn't even care if he took his next breath. It came anyway, stretching his bruised ribs with fresh pain. Today they had stripped him naked, looking for evidence of his "true" skin color. Afterward, they "forgot" to give him back his clothes.

They were watching. They always watched. What other reason would they have to keep him and Techani in the same cell? So he didn't move. If they wanted to watch, let it be as boring as possible. Let them think he had nothing left. Let them think he didn't know they would throw Techani in on top of him or that he wanted to be as much of a cushion as he could for the man. He lay there, exactly as he'd landed, letting the stone floor suck away what heat he had just to spite them. Those royal asses. They were everything his mother had warned him about and then some. They were worse than the corporate pits he'd run into back home.

The door opened, letting in just enough light for him to see where the blanket was. One blanket today, on the floor by the pit. A moment later, Techani landed on his back. Skin to skin with only a layer of drying blood between them. Murphy bit his tongue to stay silent as the tormentors laughed at the two of them.

"Are you alive?" Murphy asked after the clang of the door died away.

"Mmmm..." Techani rolled off with a slight gasp.

"They hurt you."

"Left thigh." Techani groaned. "It might be our lucky break."

Murphy went to get the one blanket they had before groping for the other man's left thigh. It took every ounce of will power to keep from gagging over the amount of blood before he found the wound. This time there was something still stuck in the lesion.

"What...?"

"They broke the knife in my thigh. You have to pull it out."

Murphy poked at it a bit more to get a feel for what he had to work with. His hands and the knife were slick with blood already. "Won't you bleed more?"

"Just be ready to apply pressure."

Murphy wrapped as much of his hand around the knife as he could. It had to hurt, but Techani gave no sign of it, thank the stars. One, two, pull. It came out easily. His other hand felt the gush of warm blood. He held the blanket against the wound with his other hand.

"What do I do with it?"

"Give it to me. Then tie off the wound."

Murphy did. It was easy enough to rip the thin blanket into a bandage. But that left them with only half a blanket to share for warmth. At least they had the one this time. Murphy nestled close to Techani to share what heat they had.

"Techani?"

"I'm alive."

"Why do they think I'm the prince?"

There was silence just long enough for Murphy to think Techani wouldn't answer.

"Because they think I'm the prince's protector."

"But you aren't."

"I was, until you came along."

It took a moment for the meaning to become clear. Trevor was Tristan. Emalynn was traveling with her own brother and didn't even know it.

"Why don't they just test my DNA? They have to have the prince's full genome on file somewhere."

"Because they can't access the profile without identifying themselves. Lord Leblanc may be royal, but he's not trying to *save* Tristan."

"But my DNA is on file too. Couldn't they check it against my parents at least? No one would know what they were doing?"

"Are your parents the kind who would submit to a random

DNA test?"

Of course not, they'd pitch a fit. "How can we prove we aren't who they think we are?"

"Just go to sleep."

Sleep came easy to his abused body. With it came the dreams of interrogations and torment. He dreamed of escape too. So it was a disappointment to wake to the guards' grip on his arms as they dragged him out into the bright lights again. This time, they dropped him almost immediately.

"What the hell?" one of the guards yelled.

The light was too much for him to see clearly, but one of the guards was on the ground next to him. Murphy scrambled over to find the woman unconscious. There was blood on her pants and head. And she still had her stunner on her belt. There were sounds of movement behind him, but all he could think about was that stunner. He moved slowly, inching his way toward her belt. Then he grabbed it.

Someone grabbed his hair and yanked him back. He almost lost the stunner.

"What are you doing?" The woman came face to face with him.

Murphy pushed the stunner into her chest and pulled the trigger. She shook with the shock, gripping his hair even tighter. When he released the trigger, she fell, pulling him down on top of her. His vision cleared enough to see a stack of guards at Techani's feet. Techani threw him a jacket.

"Out, now."

They moved through the halls at random. Techani may have been looking for something, but Murphy struggled to keep moving. He'd never been an athlete.

"In here." Techani pushed Murphy through a door. "There should be a sewer opening. Tell me when you've got it open."

This room was darker than the halls, but not black like the cell. Finding the sewer was easy. Getting the grid off needed more strength than Murphy had. He could find nothing to give him leverage. All he had were the stunners.

"This is a bad idea," Murphy said as he turned the stunner to a low setting. He stuck his finger in the little hole and put the stunner to his upper arm. "This is so stupid." He pulled the trigger.

His dreams were filled with the smell of sewage. Disgusting smells and strange sounds. People all around him, with warm water. What called to him was a scent of food.

"Ah, the princeling is awake. Stew always does it." The woman's voice laughed as he tried to get his eyes to work. "Resourceful little rat, you are, but close your eyes and I'll help you sit up."

A hand brushed across his face, forcing his eyes to close. Then a strong arm slid under his shoulders and lifted him. He felt the soft support of pillows behind him.

"You can open your eyes now."

Murphy opened his eyes, but there was nothing there. Something smelled wonderful, making his stomach reach out through his throat to get at it. The moment something touched his lips, instinct took over.

"Just like a little bird."

"Would you make up your mind, Mahini? Is he a rat or a bird or a little baby?" Techani's voice was a welcome sound in all this confusion.

"He is a little of everything," Mahini answered. "What do you expect bringing this boy to me like this and calling him your ward. I know who you are. This is not your ward."

"He is now."

Murphy didn't care what they were arguing about just so long as the food was put in his mouth. When his open mouth wasn't filled, he tried to find the spoon for himself. That's when he noticed his hand was made of pain.

"No, darling, you're still recovering." Gentle hands guided him back to a neutral position. "Didn't anyone ever tell you stunners are dangerous? With the state of your body, it's a wonder you didn't kill yourself."

"Wha...?" Murphy couldn't get his voice to work.

"You stunned yourself and broke every bone in your hand and a couple others too. I have to take Techani's word that it was necessary, but I'm still not so sure about that. In the meantime, the doctor will be here tomorrow and I need to get you ready to be treated."

"Ah..." Murphy kept his mouth open, just waiting for the stew. Mahini could say anything she wanted about him as long as the stew filled his mouth.

"Oh, and there you go distracting me. Out of here, you crazy man. You have a lot of recovering to do, young one."

She shoved a spoonful of stew into his mouth.

#

Tristan went to bed exhausted and happy every night. Work in the colony was hard, but fun was exhausting. Most of the time, Tristan couldn't tell the difference. They treated him as an equal, even when he didn't know what he was doing. Even the sheep accepted him as just another colonist. The only oddness was sleeping in the same bed with Emalynn, but he was getting used to that.

Emalynn and Darryl slipped into colony life just as easily. Emalynn became a teacher when they saw how easily the children accepted her. The adults found her knowledge of martial arts equally valuable. Darryl joined the other children in running wild. Tristan couldn't help but smile when he thought about the life they were making. This was what life should be.

Once, just once, he wished for his tablet. Seeds needed planting, and he didn't understand why they were all different. Mav caught him staring at the bins of peas.

"You can stare at them or you can ask me what's on your mind."

He got over his fear of questions and learned. When to plant peas versus corn. How to get potatoes to eye. That the colony was still under contract, though not expected to produce yet. The colonists were in debt for their lives for generations to come. No one cared that they weren't allowed to leave. Tristan agreed with them.

His favorite time of day was stopping by the schoolyard after a day in the fields. Three weeks had become routine.

Darryl was digging in the sand with a little wooden shovel, splattering it all over his companions. Each time the sand flew, they all giggled.

"Sometimes I think they do that on purpose, just so it will be harder for us to wash them up for dinner." Emalynn had slipped into place beside him on the interior of the yard. She looked so natural among the men of the school. Of course she did; she could be anything she wanted to be.

Darryl, too, happily flipping sand as though that had been his whole life. What of his father? A man with a problem. One that Tristan could solve by being a brat. So many consequences. He was a brat to bring Mal along. A brat, stamping his feet, to go to a mall. So many life changes for a boy that had nothing to do with it. If he hadn't pitched a fit...

"You're doing it again," Emalynn said.

"What?"

"You're thinking about 'what if.'"

He nodded.

"We need to be more like him."

He nodded again. "We aren't who we used to be."

"We aren't who we used to be." It was their mantra for when things got difficult. "Now, get in here and get your son cleaned up for dinner."

He laughed and started around to the entrance gate. "Will it make any difference?"

"Do you want to try to clean out the sand after he's put the potatoes in his hair or before?"

He threw his hands up in surrender. Darryl squealed to see him and flipped the sand even higher. A new game was started, which Tristan lost almost immediately. He did manage to get in, grab Darryl, and get out. However, he was now in as much need of a de-sanding as Darryl.

"Why do you like to get so dirty?" Tristan asked as he carried Darryl to the washbasin.

"Dirty," Darryl said.

Tristan tipped him over to shake out as much of the sand as he could before adding water.

Darryl giggled at the game. "Dirty." He leaned back again to be shaken again. And again and again until Tristan couldn't handle it anymore.

He'd just finished scrubbing off the dirt when Charron came running up to him. "Get Lynn and get out of town."

"What? Why?"

"There's a royal shuttle coming in for a landing. You aren't here, got it?"

Tristan nodded and turned back to find Emalynn already running for the machine yard. Mav and Chris were there with a crate of supplies.

"Go south. The jungle gets dense faster that way." Chris pressed a paper book into Tristan's chest.

Emalynn slid into the pilot's seat and started the machine without even waiting for Tristan to get Darryl buckled in. They were moving before he could even get to his seat.

"A royal shuttle? You don't think...?" Emalynn didn't take her eyes off the view out the front window.

"I don't know what I think." Tristan pulled out the paper map. "There's a river about a hundred kilometers south. The trees will be taller and fuller there."

They rode in tense silence until the paths became unfamiliar. Emalynn steered carefully between the trees, keeping their movement hidden from anyone overhead.

"Did you ever find out who tried to kill you?" Her voice sounded tight.

Tristan shook his head. "That wasn't my job. I was just supposed to survive and stay hidden." That didn't sound as comforting as it had when Techani said it.

"So either they're trying to contact you or..."

"Or I may be about to find out who tried to kill me."

#

EMALYNN - FARTHING MOON

Emalynn looked at the picture in the book and back to her hook again. Three days of camping by the river and all she'd succeeded in doing was drowning a bunch of worms. Darryl had taken to finding the worms with great zeal if not skill. Tristan had about as much success as she did in figuring out the concept of fishing from the one little paper book they'd found in the miscellaneous supplies.

Fishing was supposed to keep their minds off the village and what was going on there. Three days was making her paranoid. The royal guard should have made short work of the village and been gone or out looking for them, which they would have noticed by now.

"Cheese sandwich?" Tristan snuck up on her. He laughed. "You've been thinking again."

"You haven't?"

"Tell me your story and I'll tell you mine."

She took the offered food and turned back to watching the river. "They're all dead and it's just a matter of time before the grid search gets to us." She nibbled at the bread.

He dropped into the grass next to her. "They were arrested. Now we are abandoned on this planet with no one to help us figure it out."

"How long do we wait?"

"As long as the food holds out. They gave us more than a month of provisions. If we find more, we could be out here for a couple of months."

They'd already stretched their food a couple of days with wild potatoes.

"Do you ever just wish you could stop running?" Emalynn asked. "I mean, wouldn't it be great if we knew who was back there chasing us from our lives? We could turn around and face them."

Tristan sighed. "I don't know if I want my old life back."

"What?"

Tristan was still staring out at the water. "I like this life. It feels more like my life than the royal palace ever did. I don't know if I want to go back."

"But we don't have this life anymore either. We aren't living in the village; we're out here hiding from someone we've never even seen." Her own dreams of stability didn't include the palace. "I don't care where we go or what we do. I just want to stop running. I want to find a life that can be mine until I run out of breaths."

His eyes had dropped from the horizon to his toes. There was no getting through to a boy. They just couldn't see the logic in some things.

"If we go back now, we put them in danger."

He was right. She set aside her sandwich and tossed the hook back into the river.

"I've never liked running away."

He nodded.

"Most of my life, that's what we were doing. Every semester, Baba took me to a new colony, a new school. I never knew who she was afraid of. Then she found the apartment on Richtan. I got to stay with my class for two years before she..."

Tristan put his hand on her knee. "I'm sorry."

They stared out at the river, each lost in their own thoughts. Emalynn wished Darryl would wake up. He was so much more distracting than fishing.

"*Come back.*"

Emalynn dropped the stick she was using to fish.

Tristan looked back at the transport. "The radio."

Darryl started screaming from his crib in the back of the transport.

"Lynn and Stan, you can come back." Mav's voice was just barely recognizable through the static.

Emalynn made it to the receiver first. "We'll be there as soon as we can."

They drove the transport as fast as they could through the untamed wilderness back to the village. They arrived just in time for storytelling around in the cookhouse. Charron had saved dinner for them and Cecil took Darryl off to bed.

Mav pushed plates of roast pork and vegetables into their hands. "Come, sit. We'll talk and find out what happened."

Before she even managed to taste the pork, they were peppered with questions. "What did you do out there?" "Did you figure out how to fish?" "Was the book any good?" "Why is Lord Leblanc looking for you?"

"Lord Leblanc?" Tristan set aside his plate while his face drained of color. "He was here?"

"Oh, not his royalness himself." Chris stood to act out the horror of such a thought. "He just sent his costumed monkeys. I mean, his royal guard and that pomp of a woman, *Ma'am*. For all she said, that might actually have been her name. She was looking for some kid who matched your description. Say, has anyone ever told you the two of you could be twins?"

Emalynn couldn't taste her meal anymore. What she had eaten turned to lead in her stomach.

"They were looking for us?"

"No." Mav pulled Chris back to her chair. "Just one of you. Though it wasn't clear which one."

"But since she didn't know anything about your darling Darryl,"—Charron took up the story at that point—"we knew she was lying."

Everyone sniggered at that. Emalynn looked at Tristan and saw her fears reflected in his eyes.

"And someone"—Mav winked at them—"dropped a bucket of water on the computer just before they arrived. So it took them a while to believe our paper records."

"Lucky for you, the emergency transport was never entered into the paper inventory." Chris smiled broadly. "Heh, and we showed them Dave's grave when they asked after the crashed shuttle in the Western Forest. The barbarians dug him up to run their scanners over him only to decide that he wasn't who they were looking for."

Their distrust of the authorities ranked right up there with Baba and the smugglers she grew up with.

"Thank you," Emalynn choked out. "We couldn't have expected this."

"You're right." Charron had become serious, a cue for the rest of the colonists to find something else to do. "You've been very helpful since you came, so we gave you the benefit of the doubt. Now it's time for the truth."

Gravity doubled under the weight of Charron and Mav's

gazes. All Emalynn could do was nod.

"I'm the one." Tristan's voice shook. "Lord Leblanc is looking for me."

The women nodded as though that was expected but left the silence in place until Tristan continued.

"He knows—I don't know how—that I survived the assassination."

"The only reason he isn't trying to kill me too"—Emalynn took over—"is that he doesn't know I exist. He doesn't know about Darryl or that I'm Tristan's twin."

They were still just nodding with that expression teachers used when they knew you weren't done confessing.

"We came here to hide. If you didn't know who we were, you wouldn't be in danger. That's what we thought."

Hot tears burned paths into her cheeks. They'd brought danger to these people. They ruined a peaceful life just by being here. How many more ways could she go against everything Baba had taught her?

"Hot damn." Chris was still standing in the door. "A royal, a pair of royals, ready and willing to get their hands dirty. Never in my wildest dreams."

"Chris!" Mav went to push the other woman out.

"They weren't looking for the prince." Charron softened her voice, pulling the two of them into a motherly conference. "They were looking for an orphan accused of setting the bomb. Lynn, they were looking for you."

Emalynn's cheeks went cold.

"One more thing you need to know. They kept referring to Murphy. I get the impression this Murphy is the one who sent them here."

"No." Emalynn shook her head. "No, he wouldn't. He couldn't." *If he did, it wasn't willingly. What in the name of all the stars was he doing?*

"Who is Murphy?"

Emalynn tried to answer. She opened her mouth, but her voice had fled.

"Murphy was her boyfriend."

Charron pulled them into a hug. Emalynn went limp in the older woman's arms. Tears soaked into her shoulder.

"We have to call a council." Charron spoke softly. "The people have to know what kind of fight we're getting into."

CHAPTER THIRTEEN

TRISTAN – FARTHING MOON

Tristan found the council process here fascinating. Everyone was allowed to speak, no matter their age. This drew the process out for four days. Four days of hearing everyone's opinion of the lies they had told and their explanation. As members of the colony, they would also be given a chance to speak, but not until everyone else had made their opinions clear. The people didn't see it as a simple black and white. There were degrees and shades so it was impossible to put them in camps and count the votes.

This process was nothing like the rules of governing that his tutors had insisted were universal. At the same time, having to listen to everything made him really think about what they had done and what they were looking for.

They had lied about who they were and brought danger to the colony. The royals came and left. Maybe they would stay away now that they'd failed to find them. Or maybe not. But Tristan and Emalynn had proven their worth as citizens of the colony. Some said they should be forgiven for being in obvious trouble. Others wanted their kind of trouble to just go away. Still, others thought that they should stay but face sanction for their misdeeds.

"Tristan." Griffen pulled Tristan back to the moment. "Are you ready to speak for yourself?"

"Not really." He took his place at the head of the room. *Something please interrupt this meeting.*

"First of all, I am sorry I lied. I've become so used to lying I almost forget who I really am. We came here seeking a place to hide. I thought if you didn't know who I was, I could be safe here. I wanted a new life. One that I could call my own and not have to worry about assassinations. I didn't know you then. Now I see that I could have asked for sanctuary here and found it without lies."

A strange sound came from the office behind the council table.

"I also apologize..."

The sound came again.

"Sorry, I'll be right back." Charron left the table.

Tristan stood awkwardly in the speaker's circle. No one told him to go on. Emalynn shrugged at him. Whispers spread among the rest of the colonists, growing in volume.

Charron poked her head out of the door. "Emalynn, does your Murphy call you 'Ly?'"

Emalynn's face drained of color. "Um... yes."

"Hold on." Charron disappeared again for a second before poking her head back out. "Give me a good question for him."

"Ask him who sits on top."

"Who sits on top?" Charron asked with the maximum amount of skepticism possible.

"The answer should be Karen, and he won't have to think about it too long."

Even Tristan was confused. He looked a question at her. She answered him with a few shakes of her fists. That didn't help.

Charron came back now. "There's another shuttle on approach. This one asked permission to land and help doing so." She was speaking to the whole room. Then she looked directly at Emalynn. "The pilot claims to be your Murphy. He was able to give the correct answer with only enough of a pause to laugh. Get in there and guide him down, then tell us about Karen."

Emalynn ran to the office. She came out a very short time later with tear-streaked cheeks and a smile big enough for the whole village. "He didn't know about the autopilot." She laughed.

"Karen?" Charron prompted.

"My best friend and co-captain of the cheer squad. She's also the smallest member of the squad so she's always the top of any build." She didn't seem to notice the polite laughter around them. "He's all right." She hugged Tristan so tight he thought he wouldn't be able to breathe again for a week.

"How did he find us?" Tristan gasped into Emalynn's ear.

"I don't know, but I'm sure we're going to find out."

"Can we trust him?"

"Yes." She finally released him. "You don't believe me, do you?"

116

"I do." He lied.

"No, you don't, but you will." She held him by the shoulders and smiled. "Come, you'll want to be here when he lands."

"Are you sure about that?"

"He's been traveling with Techani, right? What doesn't he already know?"

"That I'm the prince."

"So we won't write it on your forehead. It's not like he knows I'm the princess."

He had to laugh. Her excitement was contagious. He let her drag him out to the landing field just as the shuttle passed overhead for the first time. It was a small one, a lot like the one they crashed.

"You don't think he's going to crash, do you?"

Emalynn laughed. "No, he's using the autopilot."

#

Murphy - Farthing Moon

Murphy gripped the edges of the console as the shuttle shook and lurched its way through the atmosphere. His imagination insisted that the shuttle was falling apart around him. If this was what it meant to be a shuttle pilot, he didn't want to be one.

The view showed trees reaching out to grab the shuttle and spin it off course. No, that was just his imagination again. So were the silly little houses racing toward him. No, that was the village. The shuttle was too fast. He was going to crash. He squeezed his eyes shut, praying to the stars for a quick death.

He still wasn't looking when the door swished open. The quiet drained away to be filled with too many voices for him to hear anything. He patted his chest to be sure he was still there before releasing the safety harness. He struggled to his feet, still not quite strong enough for full gravity.

"Oh my stars, what happened to you?" Emalynn's cry was the only warning he had before she crashed into him.

"I was mistaken for the prince." He tried to hug her back.

She set him down, gently, and stood back to look at him.

"Who would mistake you for the prince?" There was a boy who looked a lot like Emalynn standing next to her, holding a toddler.

"Can we go somewhere private to talk about that?" He looked at the now quiet crowd of people staring at him. Some were smiling; others were more hostile.

"Of course, dearies," said an older woman with leather-like skin and silver-white hair. "Use the council room. We've all got work that's been neglected for too long." She started shooing people away. "Take all the time you need."

It didn't take long for the crowd to disappear. There was an awkward silence between them until the last of the villagers was out of sight.

"Tristan..." She looked at Murphy while she said his name. "Will you show Murphy in? I'm going to grab some soup." Emalynn took off before either of them could say anything.

Tristan smiled. "So you're Murphy?"

"Yeah."

Tristan led him into a long low building. One high table stood with curves of benches facing it. Everything was made of wood. Unrelenting design, from the floor to the ceiling and everything in between.

"Why here?" Murphy asked. "Of all the places you could go, why here?"

Tristan's expression hardened in a scowl. "Because we thought no one would be able to find us."

Murphy felt a wave of guilt. He'd messed up again.

"Sorry."

"What are you doing here?"

"I..." What could he say? *I wanted to track down my girlfriend so I could drag her back to my parents, where she could be cleaned up a presented to the mourning monarchs as their long-lost daughter.* That didn't sound like a good way to break the ice with the prince. "I just didn't want to lose her."

"Shouldn't you have stayed with her?"

"Tristan." Emalynn stood in the door, staring daggers at her brother. "You can be nice about it."

Tristan stared back for only a moment before bowing his head.

"He has a point." Now she was looking at Murphy with those same dangerous eyes. "Why are you here? You were supposed to stay and explain my disappearance. Karen has got to be flipped. She's going to be a communications major. Or she was. You've spaced that for her."

Murphy opened his mouth to speak, then closed it again. An hour ago, he knew exactly what he was going to say to her. He'd known that she was going to be happy to see him and that everything would be good between them. In his mind, by now she would be kissing him, thrilled to be the princess.

"It's just... I mean... When I saw what happened to Baba, I knew you were in more trouble than you let on. Then when you beat up Cameron and Toby... You needed someone you could trust."

"I needed to know that the people I loved were safe." She pushed a bowl of soup into his hands. "Eat. You've lost too much weight."

She stared at him until he took a bite. It was like nothing he'd ever tasted. The soup tasted alive. He shoved three more spoonfuls into his mouth before pausing long enough for her to ask him anything else.

"What happened to you?"

Murphy told them the whole story—every wrong turn and stupid error.

"You brought the pirates?" Tristan exclaimed when they got to that part.

"I said it was a stupid idea." Murphy scowled, then continued on with the story. Emalynn rolled her eyes when he pointed out that Captain Barosa had transferred all her debt to him. They passed looks between them as he told about tracking them by the oxygen trail.

"Then we missed and got caught by Lord Leblanc."

"You followed us all this way and you missed that last bit?"

"Think about it for a moment. Why would I think that Ly with all her skills and a boy used to luxury would decide to hole up among the muck rakers?"

"You are an idiot." Emalynn took his empty bowl. "Those people are some of the nicest people I've ever met. They actually work harder than Baba and are more loyal too."

"You really have no right to talk about them that way." Tristan took up when Emalynn paused to breathe. "They have done more for us than we had any right to expect, just because it was the right thing to do."

"All right, I'm sorry." Murphy threw up his hands.

They sat there staring at each other for several minutes.

"So why are you here?" Emalynn asked.

Murphy took a breath to think about how to answer this time. "To bring you back to Techani."

More looks passed between them that he couldn't read. How hard of a decision could this be?

"I don't think we can come." Emalynn reached across

to hold Tristan's hand. "We're making a life here. We can't just leave."

#

EMALYNN - FARTHING MOON

Emalynn lay in bed, staring at the rough ceiling. She hadn't noticed how much she missed Murphy until he was standing there in front of her. He should have stayed with his aunt and finished their project at school. That's what boyfriends do, according to the vids. But vids aren't so accurate about real life adventures. She'd seen all the differences between her own life as a smuggler and what they showed on all the crime dramas. So she shouldn't be surprised that he followed her.

What was she supposed to do with him?

He claimed that he hadn't told Lord Leblanc anything. But how would he know if he'd been followed? Who knew what the Lord would glean from the little details that would come out whether you wanted them to or not. If you get enough details, you can learn just about anything. It worked best when they came from different sources.

Lord Leblanc had specifically mentioned Murphy when he came looking for them. No, that wasn't quite right. Lord Leblanc had come looking for her, but not by name. What had Murphy told him?

The thing that troubled her most was Murphy's request. Why did he care whether they went back to the monarchy? He'd found her now, in a place that was about as safe as you could get. They should be able to live out their lives in peace. Someone else could be queen. She was happy being a mom and teacher.

"Psst."

Emalynn sat up.

"Psst." It came again from outside.

Emalynn slipped out of bed, doing her best not to let Tristan feel the movement of the blankets.

"Psst."

"Who's there?"

"Mav."

Emalynn slipped out into the night. The planet overhead cast a gentle blue light over everything.

"Can't sleep, can ya, girl?"

Emalynn shook her head. She bent down to pull on her

shoes. There must be something useful she could do this time of night.

"Two boys is never a comfortable situation. Even when one is your brother. Want to talk it out?"

It was like opening the floodgates. All the insecurities and doubts tumbled from her lips while she followed Mav down the eastern path. She talked in circles, first hating Murphy, then loving him unconditionally. Tristan was just as much of a problem. The choices they set up were so stark. Couldn't she just disappear into the colony and live a quiet life?

"Well," Mav said when Emalynn's words died away. "What do you want to do?"

What a heavy question to ask so lightly. "I... I don't know. I want to stay and live the life we've made here, even though it started as a lie. But we've been found and that will only make the whole colony a target."

"Mm-hmm"

"I don't want to be queen. I don't want to face all of that... that responsibility. I mean, running the whole government, I'm not cut out for that. I'm just a girl."

"You are more than just a girl."

Emalynn rolled her eyes. "Okay, so I like helping out around here. I want to make the colony better."

"What about other colonies?"

"It would be nice, but what can I do?"

"Nothing if you stay here."

Emalynn stopped dead in her tracks. "You want to get rid of us?"

Mav kept walking. "I didn't say that. You don't have to stay here to help us. Nor does leaving mean you can't come back. There are more options out there, if you just think about it."

Mav was the gruffest woman on Farthing Moon. This was not the kind of advice Emalynn expected from her. Her surprise must have shown on her face.

"Look here, girl. You have the chance to make a huge difference in the universe. You know things the royals have forgotten. If you get out there and tell people even half of what you know, you'll be making the universe a better place. And if you get out there and tell them all that, then say, 'Good-bye, I'm going to live where they know what I'm talking about,' they'll really listen. I can't say we won't miss you terribly if you leave, but we won't hold you here. You have skills, girl. Skills that have kept you alive for this long when so many others would have lain down and died. You will get through this. Now, the sheep are easiest to shear if you catch them while they're asleep."

Emalynn laughed. That was the Mav she expected. They managed to fill eight sacks with wool before Tristan found them.

Murphy was ecstatic when he found them loading the shuttle for take off. "What changed your mind?"

Emalynn smiled. "Shearing sheep in the middle of the night is a great way to make up your mind." She kissed him lightly as she passed.

It didn't take long to load all their possessions and the crates of produce Mav insisted they would need.

"Um... where are you planning to go?" Murphy watched the crates being loaded while Cissel re-bandaged his hand.

"You said you had a rendezvous with Techani?" Tristan asked.

"Yeah."

"We'll start there." Emalynn joined them. "After that..." She shrugged.

Murphy looked at them with confusion. "But, you're going back to the monarchy, right?"

Emalynn looked at Tristan. They shrugged at the same time and went back to packing. "We're going out there to make a difference. Who knows where that will lead?"

Too soon it was time to say good-bye. Everyone was there to wish them safe travels. Emalynn was already in tears when she came to Mav, who was holding Darryl.

"Ma ma?" Darryl lurched over to be held by Emalynn.

She held him tight. "I'm going to miss you, little man," she cooed at the boy. "But Auntie Mav is going to take care of you until I put the universe back together. You be a good boy."

"Ma ma stay."

"I have to go. You stay."

"Ma ma stay!" he cried. It was enough to break her heart as she pried his fingers out of her hair and handed him to Mav. Darryl screamed as they entered the shuttle, making it impossible to keep her eyes clear. She'd wanted to smile and wave, but that wasn't going to happen now.

"We'll be back." She promised the little boy as she belted herself into the pilot's seat. "We'll fix the universe and come back for you."

CHAPTER FOURTEEN

TRISTAN – LONG-RANGE SHUTTLE

Tristan stared at the starscape on the front view screen, wishing something exciting would show up. The little shuttle wasn't going fast enough to show the shift in the stars. On the royal transport, he would have been taking a lesson right now. Or going over reports from the next colony. He even missed playing with Darryl. He especially missed that little guy, even changing his diapers.

"What's wrong?" Murphy asked without looking up from the tablet.

"Nothing," Tristan said.

"Then quit sighing."

Tristan sighed again just to see Murphy wince. He leaned over to see what Murphy was doing, but he shifted to hide the screen.

"What're you doing?"

"Trying to make us untraceable."

"That wasn't covered in your basic hacking classes?"

Murphy scowled. "You'll never make it as a comedian."

Tristan stuck out his tongue at Murphy and went back to watching the stars creep slowly across the view screen. He reached for his tablet to look up the constellations from this perspective but thought better of it. Even something that innocent could be traced if someone were looking. Uncle Phillip would have people looking. He shouldn't be surprised that his uncle was behind this. Who else would gain by killing him? Sure, there were plenty of peasant rebel groups, but they were watched too closely. Besides, they were more interested in massive public disruptions where they could use the media attention for their issues. The lords had their own agendas...

The proximity alarm jarred Tristan awake. He leaned forward to see that a small ship was in the outer range of their sensors.

"What did you do?" Murphy made it sound like Tristan had failed again.

"Found a ship." Tristan resisted the urge to stick out his tongue out. He centered the display on the ship and tried to zoom in to see what they were dealing with.

"Well, don't just announce that we're here." Murphy leaned into the controls.

Tristan cut the copilot's controls and switched to manual drive.

"What the hell?"

"What?" Tristan didn't look at Murphy. He kept his smile of triumph hidden while he fiddled with the display controls.

"You locked me out."

"Yeah. I've got this. No need to worry your pretty little head about it."

"You fuck."

Tristan shrugged. These controls weren't what he was used to, so finding the limiters was going to take some time.

"You are going to get us killed, or worse—captured. Let me drive."

"What? Just because I'm not going to lie down like a pansy and let you dictate how things are going? I may not have had the education at the fine institutions you went to, but I'm not a dummy."

"You are such a clam."

"Mirrored."

He found the camera specs. The limiters would be close in the code.

"Are you trying to impress Ly? It's not going to work."

"Just get over yourself." Tristan couldn't believe he'd actually said it. It felt rather good.

"Get over myself? You're the one who thinks he's all that just because his parents have some highfalutin job. Talent doesn't come like that."

"Don't bring my parents into this."

"Ooh, a sore spot?"

"Both of you, shut up." Emalynn was standing over them. "I can't leave you two alone for a minute without you pulling them out for a quick measure."

"We weren't titty knocking," Murphy whined. "He—"

"Well, what would you call it, then? Sitting here insulting each other's parents."

Tristan clamped his mouth shut and focused on the subroutines in the camera controls. He found what he was looking for. He remapped the controls and ran a reset on the cameras. The display shimmered for a few seconds, then resolved to show two ships approaching each other.

"Geez, you couldn't pull an evasive?" Emalynn bumped Tristan out of the pilot's chair.

"Check the distance." He reached over to toggle that part of the display.

Emalynn and Murphy looked up at him with their mouths open. Emalynn recovered first.

"How did you?"

Tristan shrugged. "They never set cameras or sensors at their true range. I figured that years ago. It took a little longer to learn to recode them."

From here they could see that one ship was a fighter type, with its gun ports open. The other was a simple transport.

"Hey, that's Techani's ship," Murphy exclaimed. "What's he doing?"

"Bump over." Tristan waved Murphy out of the copilot's seat. "Emalynn, could you give me control?"

Emalynn gave him a look but released the controls.

Now that he'd found the camera codes, it was nothing to find the limiters for all the other sensors. A few commands later and the screen split to show both sides of the communication between the two ships.

"We're just transporting these children to a world where they will be welcomed," an old woman was saying. She had short, curly white hair and a kind look in her wrinkled face.

"I don't care what you claim to be doing." The woman on that side was all business in a royal uniform. Tristan recognized the Leblanc crest on the lapel. "If you have an escaped criminal on board, we have the right to detain and search your ship."

"Children?" Emalynn asked.

Murphy nodded. All the color drained from his face.

"And Techani is on that ship, you're sure of it?" Tristan asked. He could feel a knot forming in his stomach.

Murphy nodded again. "Her name is Mags. She helped us out when we escaped. She takes in orphans and takes them to other colonies where they are more likely to be adopted. She agreed to take us to Shorvale colony where Techani said he had friends."

"Prepare for boarding," the woman in uniform declared, and then the screens went dark and they were looking at the two ships slowly getting closer together.

The three of them stared at the screen for a moment longer.

"What are we going to do?" Emalynn barely blinked. "We have to do something."

"What can we do?" Murphy asked.

A flash of light filled the screen. When it was gone, there was only one ship left. Tristan wanted to believe it was just a glitch in the sensors. There had to be two ships still. There was a glitch that made one of them look like a cloud of debris.

A new signal came from the remaining ship. Tristan hit record even before he got the image onto the screen.

"Lord Leblanc, the Eminary has been destroyed with all hands as ordered. There are no life pods or other escape vessels detected. We will remain in the area until the shuttle returns. We will transmit the records for your approval immediately following this message."

The recording stopped with a slight beep when the signal closed. Tristan couldn't bring himself to look away.

#

Emalynn – Long-range Shuttle

Emalynn stared at the screen. It couldn't be real. There had to be something wrong with the display. That wasn't real either. That ship and all hands—all those tiny hands—were gone. In all her travels with Baba and all the messy deals she wasn't supposed to know about, she'd never seen anything like that. She's seen women gunned down in cold blood for failing a contract. She'd seen people left to drift in an escape pod when they'd betrayed the boss. She'd seen smugglers disable a ship in the middle of Other space. This, this couldn't have happened.

No, this happened. Those lives were lost because they were seen to be protecting her and the boys. The only thing she could do was survive. She set a course at right angles from the one that would have brought them to the rendezvous point and got them out of that system. Then she opened the star charts and found the next inhabited system in that direction.

She spared a moment to look at the boys. They were both staring at the screen with tears running down their cheeks. She wiped away her own.

"It's over." She kept her voice soft.

Neither of them moved.

"There will be time for mourning later. For now we have to plan."

"How can you be so cold?" Tristan curled up on himself. "Didn't you see...? You know..."

"I know." She reached over to caress his shoulder. "They died for us, so we have to survive."

That got Murphy's attention. "Why? What can we do?"

"We can live. Those lumps were too intent on their evil to notice we were there. So here we are. Whatever plans we had are gone, but we have the chance to come up with something new." She reached across Tristan to offer her hand to Murphy. He gripped tighter than she expected.

Murphy pulled her closer. She pulled him to his feet and let him rest against her shoulder. She tugged Tristan to join them.

"We can't hide anymore." Her voice cracked as she said it. "We'll be hiding all our lives." She'd already been hiding all her life. It was time to break cover. How had Baba managed all these years with this kind of weight on her shoulders? Emalynn resolved that if Baba could keep her safe for fifteen years, she could keep the boys safe for now.

"You're a lump yourself." Murphy pushed away from her. "Were you there when we watched a ship full of children and people we loved go poof?"

"Of course I care." How could he miss that? "That's why we have to move on."

He gave her a dark look.

Tristan also lifted his head off her shoulder. "What can we do? Techani was my... our link back home."

The tears came fresh and hot. Emalynn matched Tristan tear for tear, until she couldn't stand any more. Techani, a man she'd barely met, but her last link to Baba. The pain she'd been able to keep in check burst forth.

Murphy wrapped himself around them, whispering, "I'm sorry. I'm so sorry."

#

Emalynn woke with an awful kink in her back and stiff joints. She listened for the noise that had woken her. Murphy and Tristan were still sleeping. She moved them just enough to get up. The noise came from the pilot's area. Her tablet was sitting on her chair, its screen lit with an incoming ping.

She should have let it go, let the caller leave a message, but her curiosity got the better of her. She sat on the floor, where the tablet's camera couldn't see, and tapped the accept icon.

"Murphy? Hey, are you there? Hey, Murphy, don't be a noodle."

The voice sounded young, probably a boy about their age. "He's sleeping." Emalynn altered her voice enough to confuse a voice analyzer. She wished she could see what he looked like.

"Who's there?"

"Who are you?"

"I asked first."

"Suit yourself." She reached up to turn it off.

"No, wait. I'm Davy. I'm a friend."

"And you're calling Murphy on my tablet."

"It's the last one he used. Do you have any idea how hard it is to trace that?"

"Not hard enough." Emalynn tried to think if Murphy had told her about his friend. She didn't think so. "Why'd you call?"

There was a bit of silence on the other end. Long enough that Emalynn reached up to hit disconnect again.

"Don't do that."

"Then answer me. You put all that effort in, so tell me why."

"You're a real pain."

She let her hand drift into view again.

"All right. Sheesh. We need to know how Murphy is progressing on his mission."

"What mission?"

"Duh, I can't just tell you that. I don't know who I'm talking to."

"You're talking to the owner of the tablet you called."

"You're really top heavy."

"Nice try, but flattery will get you nowhere."

Tristan looked up at her and she signaled him to keep quiet and stay down. He gave her a puzzled look but didn't say anything.

"Aw shit, can't you just wake him up? And what's with all the secrecy?"

"You want to talk to him about a secret mission on my tablet and you wonder why I'm being paranoid. That's an interesting twist."

Now Murphy was looking at her with a quizzical

expression. She signaled him the same way she had Tristan, but he just shook his head. When he started to get up, Tristan pulled him back down.

"Okay, look, I get that you're paranoid, but this is ridiculous. I really just need to talk to Murphy."

"I'm going to have to call you back, Davy. Cut the connection." He was glaring at Emalynn when he said it.

Emalynn heard the connection end almost immediately.

"What the hell?" Murphy asked, breaking away from Tristan and standing up. He reached for the tablet, but Emalynn was quicker. She flipped the tablet over and put her hand on it so he couldn't pick it up.

"I have the same question. What's going on that you are calling people on my tablet so they can trace it back and call you?" Letting her voice return to normal felt odd now.

"That was Davy." He spoke as though that would make it obvious.

"Who's Davy?"

"My best friend from back home."

"And what's this mission you're on?" She shifted her position to gain a little power.

Murphy backed away. He glanced at Tristan, who was also sitting up staring at him. "I'm supposed to be finding someone for my parents. Davy's on the same mission. It'll be useful to keep him informed."

Emalynn looked to her brother, feeling his paranoia as her own. "How can we trust him? Murphy, think about it. Our one grace has been hiding, and it hasn't been going so well, now this."

"Where do you think I learned my skills? He's not going to go telling Lord Leblanc where we are. Hell, he doesn't even know about you." Murphy turned to Tristan. "We need all the help we can get."

"We can help ourselves." Tristan's voice was quiet but firm.

"You don't get it, do you, prince? You're all alone out here. You have no protector anymore."

"I'm not alone, and I'm already dead."

Emalynn jumped between the boys. "We have each other." She put her hand on Murphy's chest to hold him in place. "And we'll need more help." She looked at Tristan. "But we have to chose people we can trust."

The boys turned away in opposite directions. Emalynn sighed. She let them brood for a few minutes while she gathered her own thoughts.

"There are two things we need to do. We need to get back into royal custody. I mean really royal, not just any old lord. And we have to get Lord Leblanc in trouble so he can't come after us anymore. We can do both things with one simple campaign. We get our friends to spread the rumor that Tristan isn't dead."

"My death is the only thing I have to keep me alive." Tristan had that panicked look.

Emalynn nodded. "And who's going to believe a bunch of teenagers? Especially when they have you all over the galaxy at the same time? The point is to get the attention of the royals and get so far up Leblanc's evac he does something stupid. He'll know the rumors are true and act to counter them. That will expose him."

Murphy held up his hand while looking at the floor. "But how does that get us back to the palace?"

Emalynn smiled. "Like you said, get arrested."

They looked at her with open mouths and eyes wide.

"Are you out of your mind?" Murphy asked, while Tristan bounced on his toes, saying, "Brilliant. That's absolutely brilliant."

Emalynn smiled while they worked out details. Karen and Dom, of course, would be part of it. They were the most skilled at turning toast into something fascinating. They would add the flourish that would catch attention.

"But it doesn't have to be them alone. I have friends all over the galaxy." Emalynn thought of friends from middle school and other cheer squads.

"I've moved a lot too." Murphy put in.

"They don't all have to be friends." Tristan was just as excited by this whole thing. "Once the rumors start, we just need to make sure more and more people see me all over the place."

"Ooh... ooh... I got it." Murphy bounced just a little. "I mean, I still don't get it, but... If we put out a source of Tristan images where kids can get them, they'll splice him in. Then the gossip watchers will be really confused."

Tristan stopped bouncing to look his question at Murphy.

"They'll know that the image of you is real and that it's recent, but the splicing will hide the trace back. We just need pics and vids of you to put out there."

It was so crazy it just might work. Emalynn felt the tightness in her stomach loosen for the first time since she'd found Baba.

#

Murphy didn't see how a rumor campaign could have any effect, but it was something to do. And it gave them an excuse to call Dom and Karen.

"You total shit." Karen answered the call. "Do you have any idea what we had to go through to get our project done without you?" She told them… in excruciating detail.

"I'm sorry." Murphy couldn't say it any more. "I'm so sorry."

"Yeah, well you owe us. Big time. We all got an A."

"From Zimmer?" Emalynn let all the shock show through. "You've joked."

"We might have cast the sympathy card for what happened to Baba." Dom grinned over Karen's shoulder. "So what are you two doing?"

Emalynn glanced over at Murphy.

"Getting into even more trouble."

"Ooh, when you're done, can I make the documentary?" Dom shifted so she was next to Karen. "If it's anything like a real adventure, I could start my career without an internship."

"Start a little smaller. I have a project for you." Emalynn explained. Murphy just sat back and watched her use their enthusiasm to turn the whole thing into a game. "And if you could get anyone else you know to do the same, it would totally work."

"I don't get it," Karen said. "How is making you out to be Prince Tristan going to get you out of trouble?"

"It's not." Murphy jumped in.

"Then…?"

"Could you just trust us? We kinda need to get into trouble. I promise I'll explain it all later."

Karen scoffed, but Dom was thrilled. "I knew it. It's going to be a great story."

"No, seriously. We could get in serious trouble for this." Karen pulled Dom's shoulders to look directly into her face.

"Not likely, especially if it catches on and everyone's doing it. It'll look just like a silly kids' thing." Dom was practically bouncing.

Karen turned back to the camera. "What are you into?"

Emalynn rolled her eyes. "If I told you that, you really would get into trouble."

Eventually they agreed and set up a net folder for Emalynn to drop more images and vids for them to use. "Don't be secret about the file if others want in on the game." Emalynn signed off with a sigh. She had a dark look to her eyes that stopped Murphy from saying anything more. She shook it off. "That's just the start."

While Emalynn contacted her friends from other schools, Murphy took his tablet to the back and pinged Davy.

"Hey, did you get the drive?"

"Not yet. They want proof."

"Yeah, well, proof is coming their way if they open their eyes." Murphy explained their plan. "Any help messing up the trackback on any images would help."

Davy stared at him over the connection long enough that Murphy thought they might have lost the signal.

"Are you mad?"

"Maybe, but then things are way different than we thought. The plan doesn't even begin to cover this."

Davy shook his head. "Murph, you're in deep already. Your parents have you posted."

"This isn't like biking under the grand line." Murphy shook his head. "Posting isn't going to change anything. I'm already wanted. I've got zero choice in this. She's stubborn and it's complicated."

Davy glared.

"There's at least one lord gunning for her and who knows how many with a grudge against Baba? At this point, I'm not sure Mom's going to get the tenth crack at me."

"That's not going to fly."

"Just get the drive to a palace."

It was Davy's turn to shake his head. "You kill me."

"Love you too."

Murphy started to believe this crazy plan might work when he found the first image they hadn't made. Then more rumors they hadn't started showed up in the gossip rooms.

"Check this out." Murphy called Tristan over to look at a journal entry. "Apparently you have been sunning yourself on the remote beaches of Trallihani."

"Nice. I've got some pretty good abs." The picture in question showed a dark-skinned boy with black hair who looked a lot like the prince asleep on a beach blanket. "But I thought I was shopping at the Frigarid Mall on Regina." He flipped his tablet around to show another impostor coming out of a fashionable shoe store with a bag of shoes.

Murphy shrugged. "You really get around." They laughed.

"Nice tan." Emalynn joined them. "Any news of Lord Leblanc?"

"Nothing yet, but there are a couple of reports of royals looking into the rumors."

"Already? That's... wow, that's fast." Emalynn looked at the tablet with wide eyes. It was still showing the dark-skinned Tristan. "If they're already interested, then it might be time to send them something else to think about."

Murphy didn't like the sound of that. "What are you thinking?"

"We need something more specifically targeted at the royals. Something not public." She paced from the workstation to the pilot's seat and back. "We need someone to actually walk up to the gates of the palace and say they know who and what we are."

Tristan shot Murphy a glance filled with fear. "People do that all the time," he said. "It never gets anywhere."

"What?" Emalynn and Murphy spoke at the same time.

"People are crazy. They'll say anything if they think it will get them into the palace." Tristan shrugged.

Murphy glanced at Emalynn, but she wasn't looking at him. "But how do ordinary people get a chance to talk to the queen or king?" He set down the tablet.

"There has to be a way." Emalynn locked eyes with Tristan. Murphy wondered what they were thinking at each other.

Tristan broke the gaze first. "There is. But..." He got up and walked to the back wall. "It's dangerous and someone is going to have to actually show up at a guard station." He turned and slid down the wall until he was sitting with his knees near his ears. "There are royal agents out all the time, sometimes for years so no one knows them when they come back. They have a code that will get them heard."

Murphy waited anxiously for Tristan to continue. Instead, he just buried his head in his arms.

"Tristan..." Emalynn slid down to crawl over to him. "We need that code."

He shook his head.

"We need that code. It's our key home."

He looked up. His face was as pale as Murphy's. "If you use it, you'll end up in the cells until your story can be checked."

"Sounds safer than out here." Murphy flinched from the glare they both gave him. "What? They can't kill you in custody."

133

Emalynn rolled her eyes and turned back to Tristan. "We'll be sure to warn whoever we send. But we have to give them a hang on. Otherwise, they won't know that it's anything more than a rumor."

"Code 58." Tristan was looking only at Emalynn. "It's guaranteed to get you arrested. I don't know what will happen to someone who isn't an actual agent. I don't even know what they do to an agent."

"I know just the person." Murphy started pinging Davy already.

"That friend of yours?" Emalynn asked.

Murphy nodded. "Davy is perfect. He's been arrested before so it won't be as big of a shock, and I know he'd be willing."

It was decided, though the twins weren't so thrilled with that, but they could think of no one else who would do it. Davy wasn't all that thrilled either. When all the accusations of insanity were through, Davy agreed to get the drive with Emalynn's birth record to the palace at Rakan.

CHAPTER FIFTEEN

EMALYNN – LONG-RANGE SHUTTLE

Emalynn fidgeted with the controls. Three days of bolstering rumors and sending out fresh pics of Tristan to keep the rumors running had her on edge. It didn't feel like they were doing anything anymore. Lord Leblanc wasn't cooperating either. His movements were private.

Another proximity alarm brought her back to the present. They were entering a well-populated system with two colonies. A quick check of their vital levels showed they couldn't just skirt around them.

"Hey, guys. Where do we want to hang out for a while?"

"What do you mean?" Tristan was in front of the green screen, posing for something.

"We've got to pick a colony to land on and I'm not interested in the primitive moon colony this time. Besides, it's a lot older than Farthing Moon, so not as useful for hiding." She put the two primary world colonies up on the screen. "I can't really see much difference other than Aleppo has more islands in the tropic zone and New Brooklyn has more forest zones marked for vacationers."

"There are a number of pictures of me on the beach already. Let's go to the forest zone. We could start putting out real pictures of me."

"Not until we know what Leblanc is up to," Murphy said.

"Whatever." Tristan dropped his pose. "I think Uncle Phillip has a house on Aleppo, or a cousin. I'm not sure, but Aleppo sounds familiar."

Emalynn tapped in the coordinates. "Right, New Brooklyn it is." Now to get the landing permits. She would have to fake an adult's permission. Three ungraduated teenagers traveling alone would call too much attention.

"So I've been thinking we should have a graduation party. You know, before we have to go to our internships," Emalynn said as she pulled up one of Baba's old accounts.

"What are you talking about?"

"Cover story."

Murphy came to look over her shoulder. "Sounds like fun."

"Damn, we have to prove we have a place to stay." Emalynn complained.

"So make a reservation."

Emalynn sighed. He really didn't get the part about hiding out. She dug up another of Baba's old credit accounts in a different name and rented a cabin in the mountains. She guided the shuttle through orbit and down into the port. This time she let Tristan see that she really could fly.

Murphy's tablet alerted him to a call as soon as they were out of security.

"You're going to owe me big when this is all over." Davy started as soon as Murphy opened the connection.

"Not a secure location." Murphy walked away.

"What was that about?" Tristan asked.

Emalynn shrugged. She was looking for the transport to the mountains that came with the cabin rental. She wanted to know what was so important that he couldn't talk about around them. It bothered her more than she would let on.

"You'll want to hear this." Murphy called them over. "Davy, say it again."

"What, she still isn't going to let me see her?"

"Nope. She's paranoid and stubborn. Go ahead."

There was a bit of a silence in which Murphy rolled his eyes, then glared at the screen.

"Limp noodle." Davy's voice came through. "We've been watching the movements of various militias and house guards. There is a disturbing trend of more and more armed groups massing in the regions around Prime. From what we can see, there are at least three different militias involved, but it's hard to tell because they're hiding their IDs. They haven't made any sort of move yet."

"We can't let that stay silent." Emalynn could see the fear in her brother's eyes. "That's a coup waiting to happen and I'm sure that's not going to bode well for the people you're fighting for."

"That's what we thought, but there isn't much we can do

136

about it."

"Tell the news channels," Emalynn said. "They can't be that hard to find and there will be all kinds of questions if even the rumor of their presence gets out."

"You really like this go-public thing for everyone but yourself."

"It works for me."

Let Davy think her crazy. When he found out who he'd been talking to, he'd understand. Or not, it didn't matter.

"You sound a little too much like you know what you're doing."

"I was raised to survive, and I will survive."

"Whatever. See ya, Murph. Don't do anything I wouldn't do."

The connection went dead.

"Come on, the transport will be this way." Emalynn led them through the shuttle port, following the signs.

#

MURPHY – NEW BROOKLYN

Murphy closed the connection with Davy. The last thing Davy said made his stomach tighten into knots.

"So just sit tight and there will be others there who can handle this girl. They've seen the video so don't worry about them."

He worried over what Davy meant and how he should tell the others. Maybe he shouldn't.

"Come on, Murphy." Emalynn stood by small transport. "They won't wait all day."

"Sorry."

Emalynn just nodded. There were no seats together. Murphy took a seat next to a man dressed all in brand-new mountain clothes.

"I'm heading up to the peak of Caraway." Murphy's seatmate said. "I heard up there you can almost feel the pull of the vacuum. I've managed to save a full month's worth of vacation just so I can feel that."

"Sounds great." Murphy tried to sound bored. It didn't work. He got to hear all about the guy's job and how he didn't really like working with other people all the time and couldn't he just get that promotion already so he could spend his days checking the stats in his office rather than working directly with the clients? "You know, whatever the weather is, that's just going to be great no matter what. I'll be all alone up on the side of the mountain. So what brings you to New Brooklyn?"

"Last hurrah. I'm here with friends before we graduate."

"Oh, I wish I'd thought of that. But my parents probably wouldn't have let me go anyway. You're pretty lucky."

"That's what people tell me."

"So where are you going?"

"Not sure." Murphy lied. "Caroline booked the place." He nodded at a girl up at the front of the bus. Holy crap, he was as paranoid as Emalynn.

He was saved from further discussion when the bus pulled into its first stop. There was a lot of shuffling around as people got off and others got on. Murphy snagged a chance to move closer to Tristan.

When they pulled into their station, it was dark. Not even a stationmaster to greet them. The situation put Murphy on edge. Emalynn looked ready to fight and Tristan was making himself as small as possible.

The sound of the transport pulling out of the station made him jump.

"Isn't...?" He started.

"Shut it," Emalynn snapped.

He recognized the tiger-like look from her attack on Toby and Cameron.

Murphy clamped his mouth shut. When she waved at them to get down, he did. Tristan did too. He couldn't see or hear what she did.

Emalynn dashed suddenly to the left and put a woman on her face in the middle of the clearing. She shot another out of a tree on the other side of the clearing. Where did she get a gun?

"Run." Emalynn gestured toward the woods.

He ran. Tree roots reached for his ankles and toes in the dark. Trees jumped out at him. He kept running even after he'd lost track of Emalynn and Tristan. There were sounds of gunfire in the distance.

He pulled up short in front of a large tree. His lungs were burning and he just couldn't run anymore. Something moved to his right, so he ran left, right into a large woman. He tried to bounce away, but she caught his injured arm.

His knees buckled from the pain. Stars danced before his eyes before fading out completely.

When he came to, he was bound and lying on a crappy

mattress.

"Fuck." Nothing happened. "Fuck, fuck, fuck, fuck, fuck." He was shouting by the end.

"Shut up." Emalynn's voice came from the wall on his left.

"Where are we?" he asked.

"A camp, probably a hunting camp on Crevesha Mountain."

"Isn't that where we're going?" He tried to remember what she had told him about their reservations.

"Yeah. I'm betting this is the cabin I rented."

He could hear the dark tones of her anger seeping through the wall.

"Trevor?"

"Not here." That one came with undertones of panic.

Murphy tried to sit up, but the bindings around his wrist pulled painfully. This is what Davy had warned him about.

"Are you bound?"

"Yeah. I think they broke my hand again."

"Shit." He could hear her flopping on a creaky bed of her own.

"Don't worry about me."

"Has that line ever worked in any vid you've ever seen?"

"No."

"Shut up, both of you." The voice was deep and gravelly.

"Fuck."

"Murphy. Shut up."

Murphy bit his tongue. He'd heard that voice before. So often when his parents didn't know that he was right outside the window. He never did learn her name, but her role as an enforcer was clear from the first. Her involvement couldn't be a good sign.

Murphy drifted in and out of consciousness. He listened for anything that would give him a clue about what the army was doing. They had the princess. Why weren't they already on a shuttle heading for home?

His first clue was a lot of shouting and some gunfire. He struggled to sit up. Then he heard the engine. Then the world turned itself over several times. When he looked up, the ceiling was replaced by a clear blue sky. The only thing blocking the sight was a crane. A great green metallic beast with a horrible gaping maw just like a monster in a horror vid.

Tristan burst through what was left of the door to his little room. "Shit."

"Untie me," Murphy called out.

Tristan came over with a knife. There was a moment of

hesitation before he cut the ropes. He was back out the door before Murphy could get up.

"To your left," Murphy called when Tristan hesitated.

Tristan disappeared to the left and there was more crashing about.

Murphy eased himself to a standing position, trying out his numb feet and ankles before trying to climb over the door and ceiling bits that clogged the little room.

Emalynn and Tristan were sitting nose to nose on the bed. A wave a jealousy washed over Murphy. He'd never be that close to her. He could never be that open with her.

"Oh, Murphy." Emalynn launched herself at him, folding her arms around him and lifting him off the ground. "We have to get out of here. They know you."

"Uh-hmm," Murphy mumbled into her shoulder.

#

TRISTAN - NEW BROOKLYN

Emalynn led them out into the mountains, away from any marked path. Tristan followed for a while, but her pace was hard for him to keep up. At the first stream they came across, she dropped in her tablet. Next they came to a crevasse and she made Murphy toss his. Tristan pulled his battery before she could tell him to destroy it.

"We're going to need one."

She grunted. They walked all day without saying much.

They stopped to camp next to a stream. The water looked nice and clear, but it was so shallow it would be hard to draw without getting mud too. With no way to start a fire, they camped cold.

Something had made her pull into herself after their reunion. When she didn't talk to them all day, it was bearable. They were hiking over treacherous grounds. Now the lack of eye contact chilled him more than the mountain air.

"Ly, just listen to me." Murphy pleaded to her back. "I didn't tell Davy where we were. I don't know how they found us."

Emalynn didn't say anything.

"Emalynn?" Tristan sat beside her. "He has a point."

"It's not that." Her voice betrayed the tears she was hiding.

His chest tightened around the fear she felt.

"We have to trust each other." Tristan turned to face her.

140

"I told you it's not that." Emalynn turned away, hiding her face in her knees. "He was the safe one. He was the one who could reach out, but he has enemies too."

Tristan looked over at Murphy, who shrugged. He took the cue to back off, though.

"So what are you going to do about it?"

"I don't know."

They sat in silence for a time. Tristan tried to feel what she was feeling, but it was all jumbled up in his own mind. Murphy was the safe one, like Emalynn said. Tristan had Uncle Phillip trying to kill him. Emalynn was running from Baba's enemies. Murphy was the one they didn't have to worry about. Only now he was the target.

"There are too many enemies," Emalynn said. "There are too many and I don't know what to do."

"Who said it had to be you?" Tristan put his hand on her shoulder. "We have enemies coming from three directions. Good thing there are three of us to keep watch." His smile died on his lips.

Emalynn put her hand over his. "It's me because I have experience."

"And I have the training. Murphy isn't exactly innocent either."

She turned to look at him.

"Have you heard the stories he tells about getting in trouble? It might not have been life or death, but it's still something."

She snorted. "I guess."

Tristan looked back at Murphy and nodded for him to come over too. Murphy took his place on Emalynn's other side. Emalynn took his hand.

"I have to confess, I know who they are. I just didn't know they would be coming for me." It was Murphy's turn to hide his face in his knees. "My parents lead a rebel group known as the Alecti Army. No, let me finish. I knew about it since I was kid, and when I graduate, I'll probably join them. No offense to you, Tristan, but there are many out here who don't benefit from the current system. The army is supposed to be finding ways to get the attention of the royals. I never dreamed that my parents would send them after me just because I ran away from school."

Tristan opened his mouth, but there were no words. This trip was turning out to be very educational, but not in the way his parents had meant.

"School is important," Emalynn said. "Graduating—even more so."

"I know." Murphy looked up at the sky.

Stars were coming out across the sky. Tristan leaned back to see the pictures they made. In ancient times, people believed those pictures had meanings. They would look to the stars to tell them what to do. Tristan wished the stars were still so wise.

Emalynn leaned back to join them looking up. "So what are we going to do?"

"We're going to finish the plan and take back our throne." Tristan felt the conviction his speech masters had tried to teach him. "We've been out here among the people now. We know enough to lead them, to really lead them into a better way. We can't let that die because we're scared."

Strange how after years of practicing making speeches in the grand hall and in front of gilded mirrors, it took talking to his friends on a cold night under the stars to finally feel the power of a good speech.

"You are such a dork." Emalynn reached over to bump his shoulder. "Did your masters teach you to speak like that?"

"They tried."

CHAPTER SIXTEEN

MURPHY - NEW BROOKLYN

Three more days of camping cold before they found a village. Murphy couldn't wait for a shower and a meal that was more than nuts and berries. Preferably freshly cooked.

"It was horrible," Emalynn told the lady at the inn. She scowled at Tristan. "He insisted he knew how to navigate by the sun. I tell you, boys!"

Tristan refused to look at Emalynn. Murphy kept his eyes on the floor to keep from laughing.

"It's nothing," the innkeeper said with a laugh. "We have a room for you."

Murphy used his ID to pay and insisted on first shower for it.

"So where do we go from here?" Murphy flopped on the bed, full and happy at last.

Emalynn perched by the window. "We need to know if the drive has been delivered yet."

Tristan nodded from the comfy chair in the corner.

"What are you thinking?" Murphy looked up at her.

"If they don't have the drive yet and we get caught by the royal guard, we aren't going to be believed and there's no telling what they'll do with us. If they have the drive there, then they're probably out looking for us already."

Murphy agreed. "The only way to know would be to try to contact Davy."

They all grimaced for that. If he'd made it, would he be contactable?

"We could get the attention of the royals ourselves," Tristan said.

"You don't think we have their attention yet? Have you

been looking at the Tristan sightings?" Murphy asked.

"We don't have their attention—the gossip sites do. We need to turn it on us."

Murphy didn't see the difference. What had the point been for all those sightings?

"Ooh." Emalynn jumped up. "Code 58 will get their attention."

Tristan looked about, ready to say no, and Murphy would have agreed with him, but he closed his mouth without saying anything. Damn, it was hard to work with twins when they could think each other's thoughts like that.

"What?" Murphy asked.

"We record a vid with both of us and say 'code 58' somewhere in it," Emalynn suggested.

Murphy got it. "You mean like a 'Hi, mom and dad, don't worry about me. I'm safe and fine. Oh, and a friend of mine is going to drop off something you really need to see. It's totally a code 58.' Something like that?"

"Not that cheesy, but yeah. Something like that." Emalynn agreed.

"Uncle Philip will see it," Tristan said.

"We'll make sure it's the palace guard that gets to us first." Emalynn was pacing now. "We plan the release for when we are right next to a royal outpost. Where's the nearest palace?"

Tristan got a funny look on his face. "I think its on Aleppo."

"Nothing on New Brooklyn?"

"Maybe an office or something. But the governing seat of this system is on Aleppo." He sounded apologetic about not having a palace on both colonies.

"We're going to have to get the shuttle back." Emalynn breathed deep. "That could be a problem." She looked at Murphy.

"Did you use the same accounts to secure the docking fees and the cabin?" He knew the Alecti Army would have stopped when they found them.

"No."

"Then we should be fine. That shuttle was registered by Mags, so I don't think they traced it. They were probably tracking the tablet."

"But I used that tablet for both accounts."

"That would take days to track down, if you're good." Murphy shook his head. "I'm their best besides Davy."

"So, not impossible," Emalynn said.

"No, not impossible, but once you destroyed the tablet, it

became impossible."

"But the tablet is not the only place the information is stored." This time it was Tristan casting doubt.

"Actually, for tracking, yes, it is. No business cares which tablet sent them the information about an account. They only see and record the account information. So once the tablet is gone, there's no link between the two accounts." How he hoped that was true.

"The sooner we get back to the shuttle the better," Tristan said. "There are other things that could go wrong if we wait too long."

"First thing in the morning, then." Murphy stretched. Soon they were snuggled into the beds with the lights out. Murphy could feel sleep settling over him.

"We should record the message here." Emalynn's voice shattered the peace.

"What are you talking about?

"The message we're going to send to the king and queen. We should record it here. We won't release it until we're in a better position, but we should record it now. Have it ready." She flipped the lights back on.

Tristan groaned and pulled a pillow back over his head.

"You want to record it now?"

"Yes. Get it done. Come on, you two, get up. This won't take long."

Arguing wasn't going to do them any good. They got up.

The message was short and simple and had both of them in it. Tristan came on first.

"Hello, Mother and Father, I just wanted to let you know I'm doing well. My visit with Uncle Phillip went well, but I don't think he was ready for me to leave. Tell him I'm sorry, but I didn't want to miss my chance to meet Emalynn." That's when Emalynn joined the video with a smile and a wave. "Oh, and I'm expecting a package from a little out-of-the-way place called 'code 58.' It's probably going to get to Regata ahead of me, so just keep it in a safe place. I'll see you soon. Love you."

Murphy added the metadata that would ensure that it got posted publicly 'by accident.' He took the extra minutes to post it with a delay so they wouldn't have to worry about it. They would have twenty-four hours to get to Aleppo.

"Don't hide the location." Tristan looked over his shoulder. "If anything goes wrong, we want them to know where to come looking for us."

145

"The same could be true of our enemies," Emalynn said. "Do we want to alert them to our presence?"

"It would only matter if we get caught before the release," Tristan said. "Our enemies already know where we are."

Murphy nodded. Now they could go to sleep.

#

EMALYNN - NEW BROOKLYN

They made it back into the capital city without any trouble. For some reason that didn't make Emalynn feel any better about it. It was just too easy. The boys laughed at her when she mentioned it. Better paranoid than caught.

"We just want to get off this world," Tristan complained. "Shouldn't we be going to the shuttle port?"

"That's the most likely place for them to be looking for us."

"So how does hanging out in parks and museums help us?" Murphy asked.

"Because they have publicly accessible cameras." They just looked at her. "If we spend enough time away from the shuttle port, they'll come looking for us. Then we'll be able to slip around and get our shuttle easily enough."

"How do you know this stuff?" Tristan's voice was a mix of awe and disdain.

"Baba taught me." He gave her that same dead expression. "I've always known what she did for a living. When she started assassinations, I was scared she would get caught, so she taught me how not to get caught and how to get caught for those times when she needed to be."

"Why would she do that?" This time it was Murphy challenging her.

"Sometimes the best alibi is being in custody for something completely unrelated."

She was taking them in an easily predictable pattern through the city's attractions. She'd planned a simple route around the city based on the tourist sites for New Brooklyn. They were about halfway through the route now. More than long enough.

They came upon a group of women who were paying too much attention to the park and not enough to each other. They stopped when Emalynn did. No, that wasn't too obvious.

"Wait, let me see the tablet." She pulled them to the side of

146

the path where they wouldn't be in the way but far enough from any benches that it wouldn't seem too odd that they didn't sit.

"What?" Tristan handed over the tablet.

"Trouble. Stay alert." She tapped into the city network and found the list of cameras. She looked for all the cameras on the park and found they all appeared to be working. No, they should have been visible on two of the cameras but only showed up on one.

"What do you see?" Tristan asked after a while.

"I don't see us." She set the display to show the two cameras on this part of the path.

They didn't need to say anything. They knew they were in trouble. Emalynn nodded and they turned and walked back the way they'd come. Passing the women was a risk she had to take.

The women closed ranks to block the path in front of them. Emalynn glanced back the other way and saw the rest of the ambush team coming toward them.

"Stay close." She relaxed into a ready stance.

The boys turned back to back. Emalynn could only hope they had more skills than she'd seen. There were more adversaries than Emalynn could count. They had a tight net around them, but they wouldn't all be able to fight at once. Let them get in too close.

When the fight started, it was quick. They were trained fighters, but they were trained to use their weapons. Emalynn was able to close with the first assailant before she could charge her stunner and she knocked it into her friend just in time for the discharge. She then pulled the woman around as a shield for the next. She dropped with the discharge of her friend's weapon. That left him vulnerable. Emalynn dropped him with a quick jab to the throat, followed by an elbow to the sternum and a fist to his nose. She had just enough control to throw him at the next one. She needed to keep the fight going long enough to get the attention of local cops.

The first of the fighters stepped in close enough. Emalynn moved back to draw her further in. When she struck, she saw surprise on the woman's face. An elbow to the chest, duck, kick, grab. Emalynn didn't think in terms of opponents, but body parts. She couldn't be as aggressive as she wanted to be. Kick, grab, twist, duck, jab, shove.

Something changed. She took a moment to look around. A distraction that cost her a fist to the chest but showed there were more fighters now. It had become a general brawl. Emalynn grabbed the boys and started making holes in the fight. Kick, move, shove, grab, step, jab, twist. Then they were out.

"Can we get off this rock now?" Murphy asked.

#

TRISTAN - NEW BROOKLYN

Tristan was still shaking when they arrived at the shuttle port. He'd never really believed his security masters when they told him he would need to know how to escape. Then in less than a week, he'd used every one of those lessons. All that did was prove that his security masters had been right.

He could feel eyes on him from every angle while they waited for Emalynn to finish all the bureaucratic nonsense so they could get their shuttle back. Every noise was an assassin taking aim.

"Calm down, would you?" Murphy chided him. "If you look too suspicious, we'll never make it out of here."

Tristan did his best to stop looking around.

"Let's go. We're in bay G18." Emalynn waved them over. "We have just over an hour to get through security."

An hour. That shouldn't be too bad. Most of that they would use getting through the gates and the rest getting the shuttle ready. Still, it gave their enemies an hour to find a way to stop them.

The first gate was no problem. Tristan began to calm down a bit until they were delayed at the second gate, having their IDs checked twice. Tristan could see the tension building in Murphy's shoulders too, though Emalynn looked like everything was just fine. She smiled and thanked the guard as she passed through.

It was the final full-body screening at terminal G18 that worried Tristan. He'd hated those booths since the first time he had to use one. Now his imagination was telling him about all the things that could go wrong. Like the fact that Emalynn had been in there for three minutes already when the thing usually cycled in just one. Murphy's turn took just as long. By the time it opened for him, Tristan had to force himself into the booth.

The booth was a box just big enough to stand in while scanners stripped you naked and gave you a complete medical exam. He was sure the thing must have broken for how long it took to cycle. He had no weapons or banned substances on him. *Breathe,* he told himself. *It's reading your panic. Just breathe.* The booth door opened at last to the bay and three guards with laser weapons pointed at him.

"You will come with us," said the one in the middle.

Emalynn and Murphy were nowhere in sight. He nodded and let the woman put a hand on his shoulder to guide him.

She pushed him down a stark-white hallway right into the back of a police van. It was a short drive with two armed guards in the back of the van. They never took the guns off him. At the other end, there was another stark-white hallway that led to a cellblock with five cells.

Emalynn was in the one directly across from the door and Murphy to the right. There was an empty cell between them. Tristan hoped that would be his cell. The hope lasted all of about three seconds before he was guided to the cell opposite Murphy.

"You can't just keep us like this." Murphy's yell was muffled by the glass door of his chamber. "What did we even do? You have to tell us what we're being held for."

The guard pushed Tristan into the cell and closed the door.

"Murphy..." Emalynn's voice was just as muffled. "Shut it."

Tristan couldn't see Emalynn clearly from his cell, but Murphy was right across from him. Murphy paced the floor like a caged animal—back and forth the length of the glass front. Tristan knew the feeling. He also knew it was a waste of energy.

"Emalynn?" he called.

"I'm fine," she called back.

"What are we going to do?"

"Hope it takes longer for the system to figure out what to do with us than it takes for our parents to come looking for us." Her tone was light, but he could feel the panic below the surface.

"That's dumb." Murphy had his face pressed against the glass, trying to see into Emalynn's cell. "Are you kidding us? That's all you're planning? We at least have to get our stories straight."

"No, we don't. We're in relatively safe custody right now. Best to leave it that way." He pointed up to the cameras pointing into each cell.

"Don't worry about it. When they ask, just tell the truth."

Murphy threw up his hands and went back to pacing.

Tristan sat on the bench at the back of his cell. Their vid would release in just a few hours. How long would it take to get royal attention? One, maybe two days. They just needed to stay here that long.

CHAPTER SEVENTEEN

EMALYNN - POLICE CUSTODY

Emalynn took a deep breath. Baba had used police custody often to avoid trouble. This was just the same. As long as they were in here, they couldn't be killed. That was the theory. She took another deep breath and tried to banish all thoughts about how Baba had always planned her custody, knew what she was charged with, and all the other differences.

She tried sleeping. No use—the bench in this cell wasn't meant for that. It was a full gravity planet and there was no cushion. Even if she could have gotten comfortable, her mind would have raced on. When she couldn't sit anymore, she practiced the slower forms as best she could in the limited space. They helped her stay calm but didn't give any of the answers she sought.

When they brought around the second meal without any explanation for their imprisonment, Emalynn listened to Murphy rant at the guards. She actually enjoyed the way he barked at them as though they would listen to a scrawny boy like him and take his threats seriously. The guards just laughed at him and left them alone again.

"This is such bullshit." Murphy raged on when they had left. "What the hell is going on here?"

"They want us to talk amongst ourselves," Tristan answered.

Of course that made sense. They were being left with only the cameras and microphones to watch over them. Most people would be actively trying to figure out this whole situation. They'd talk it through, forgetting they were being recorded. That would explain the careful placement of the three. The only way for them to talk to each other would be to yell loud enough to be heard through the glass. That would also make sure any recording would pick up everything they said.

"Then let's talk and get this process over with." Murphy complained.

"Why?" She leaned her head on the glass at the front of her cell. "We're safe enough right here. Give it enough time and we'll be even safer."

"Or we could be worse off," Murphy responded. "Who's going to be the first to find us and what kind of excuse are they going to come up with to take us?"

Emalynn didn't have an answer. The knots in her stomach tightened. Slow breathing could only do so much. "So you want us to just reveal all our silly little secrets in the hope they won't call up whoever is worse? We've got nothing, Murphy. Right now, our best bet is to stay right here."

They fell into a silence that amplified her thoughts. What would Baba do? Baba wouldn't have been caught like this. They couldn't even monitor their tricks.

"Hey, Ly," Murphy called. "You remember that time when Karen was late to practice and you were all freaked out about whether you could even go on with the drills because she wasn't there when she'd promised she would be?"

"Yeah, except I wasn't freaked out."

"You were too freaked out. Anyway, what did you do that day?"

"I started teaching the girls kicks." What was he playing at?

"Your squad already had the best high kicks in the kingdom."

"I didn't teach them high kicks. We were learning the fighting kicks Baba taught me." They'd turned them into new cheer moves so Coach wouldn't be mad at them.

"You were the one who drilled your squad?" Tristan asked. "I thought you'd learned all that from being on the squad."

"I learned a lot from being on the squad, but balance and high kicks I had long before I joined."

"What about that time Dom convinced you to go out when you had a major project due the next day?"

"I was up all night finishing that damned project." Emalynn remembered the look on Baba's face when she got home. "But it was worth it. And you—trying to get Karen to finish that Bio report for you."

Murphy laughed and filled Tristan in on all the details of

how that escapade had turned out. Tristan had stories too. Even royals get in trouble when they could. Emalynn added some of her hijinks Murphy didn't know about, and he shared from times before they met. The tension let up a little as they began to giggle at the silly things they used to do. Even at the times they were caught and the adults didn't know what to do.

They were still laughing when the guards returned. Three of them this time, with the same bored looks they'd worn every time they came through that door. The laughter died when the guards marched up to Tristan's cell.

"Hold up your ID," one ordered.

Tristan must have complied because they didn't say it again. Emalynn expected them to come to her next. She was disappointed when instead they opened Tristan's cell and pulled him out. Emalynn saw the bruises on his face and arms from the earlier fight and felt a stab of guilt. They were in that ugly stage of healing.

Tristan tried to pull away. "Where are you taking me?" He got cuffed for his efforts and dragged out of the cell anyway.

"What's going on?" Murphy pounded on the glass at the front of his cell. "You have to tell us why we're here. You can't just take him away. We're together."

Tristan tried to plant his feet and twist out of their grip. "No." Emalynn saw a fresh drop of blood from a cut that had reopened. He fought until the door closed behind him. All she could do was hold her hand to the glass and cry.

Murphy screamed obscenities at them. "We can't let them do that. We can't just let them take him like that."

"What can we do? Murphy, we're locked up. What can we do?" Tears dripped from her cheeks, leaving streaks on the glass. "What can we do?"

"You can't just give up on him. He's your brother. Think of something. Fight. I don't know."

Emalynn caught up short. "What did you say?"

"You have to fight for him."

"No, you said he was my brother. How did you know that?" They'd been careful not to tell anyone what they discovered. "Murphy! How do you know he's my brother?"

"Because I know who you are. Who you really are."

Emalynn couldn't breathe. All the knots in her stomach were back, only this time they were tighter.

"I was sent to find you." His words were almost too quiet to hear. "When we realized you would be high school age by now, we sent a whole class worth of kids out to find you. I did. When I offered to help you, I figured you would go with my friends back to Calaron. My parents have been waiting for you for years."

Emalynn staggered back to her little bench. It was so hard to breathe. "You knew?" She knew it wasn't loud enough for him to hear. She didn't really want him to answer anyway. How could he? How could he have known and not told her?

"Ly? Are you okay?"

"No, I'm not okay." Her ears rang from her own volume. "You lied to me. You were never my friend. I was just a mark."

"It wasn't like that." His voice sounded full of pain. "Ly, I do like you. I have always liked you. I wanted it to be you so I could go home and we'd still be together. I would have transferred at the end of the semester anyway."

"Shut up. Shut up. Just shut the fuck up." She threw herself at the glass and hit it hard enough to make it reverberate.

They were quiet after that. She curled up on her bench and let the tears flow.

#

TRISTAN - POLICE CUSTODY

Tristan sat in the little conference room, waiting for an explanation. Waiting really for someone, anyone, to walk into the room. He'd been tossed into the room the same way he'd been tossed into his cell. The conference table and four chairs, instead of a built-in bench, were all that distinguished this room from the cell. And the possibility of talking to his friends.

"Hey. I have rights. You can't just leave me in here like this." Yelling at the walls didn't get him anywhere, but it made him feel better. He didn't even know which direction to yell. There were no panels, no blemishes that could be camera covers, no vent covers to hide microphones.

That was a thought that scared him more than anything so far. He was used to being under the watchful eyes of public cameras. He'd lived with them all his life. Nowhere to hide, just get lost temporarily while people looked for the right camera. If you were clever enough, you could trick the humans on the other side, but the cameras were always there. They watched without prejudice. They were infallible witnesses.

Panic settled into Tristan's chest, clamping down on his heart and lungs. Emalynn used the martial forms to keep

154

herself calm and ready. Techani had taught him the same thing. Starting with the ready stance, Tristan felt his chest loosen. Then the energy work and breathing exercises that were so a part of Emalynn he could feel her standing with him. He moved on to the short piece of the beginner's form that he knew. Then he did it again. Six rounds later, when he felt he could almost feel his opponent in his hands, the other door to the room opened and a man walked in.

He wasn't really anything to look at, just a man, thin— almost scrawny—in a fashionable blue business suit. Not too expensive and not really of the caliber he would have expected to see of anyone working in the royal household. He sauntered in as if trying to show he was too weak to be a danger, but Tristan had been trained to spot danger. Under that not-quite-fitted suit, the man had a weapon. There was another hidden in the boots. Possibly only stunners but possibly something far more deadly. His chest tightened again.

"What are you?" Tristan demanded with all the arrogance he could muster. He saw a flash of surprise cross the man's face.

"My name is Dominick. I've come to take you home."

"I don't want to go home." Tristan knew this man could not be trusted.

"Sire, your identity is known." He wore a mask of concern, holding out his hands to Tristan. "It's time to come back where we can keep you safe."

Tristan backed away. "Did Lord Leblanc send you?"

"Your uncle is concerned for your safety."

Now he had proof. "I don't want to go home. I'm happy living as a pauper."

"Sire, you can't mean that. Think of your parents."

The man pulled out a chair to sit at the little table. Tristan knew the polite thing would be to join him. It was expected. It would make him even more vulnerable than he already was. Tristan moved closer to the door he'd been shoved through. He wished for the glass barrier of the cell.

"If my parents are that concerned, they can come and get me themselves." Tristan decided to give the man an out and see if he would take it.

Dominick, if that really was his name, swallowed hard and breathed six deep breaths. "Be reasonable, sire. Your father can't be away from the duties of state for that long. It's all done anyway. That was the reason for the delay. You've been transferred into my custody. We're just waiting for the transport to get here and we'll be off. You'll be home safe and sound within a few days and back to your studies even sooner."

"I'm not going with you." Tristan called on his reputation as a brat from childhood. His nannies had done everything they could think to break him of it, but it had worked more often than not back then.

"You don't really have a choice, sire."

"Then you don't know me all that well. Guards, I want to go back to my cell now. This man is not my legitimate guardian and I will not go with him." He didn't really expect anything to happen with that. What he got was a bit of a shock.

Dominick pulled the projectile gun from his jacket and pointed it directly at Tristan. "None of that now, sire." Suddenly the word sire sounded more like an insult than an honorific.

Tristan dropped to the floor and rolled under the table. He managed to catch Dominick off guard enough to bite his ankle and get his hands on the second weapon. What he found was a mini explosives cannon. More than just a projectile weapon, it could be loaded with enough explosives to turn the entire police station into fine powder.

Dominick regained control of himself and kicked Tristan in the face. Tristan tried to crawl away through the field of stars that had erupted around his head. Enough of them were blood-red to tell him he was bleeding. Best to just ignore it but harder than it would seem. He knocked the table over and pointed the cannon over the side at Dominick. Dominick's eyes went wide in terror.

"Sire, don't use that."

"What, this little explosive cannon that isn't legal in any of the colonies? Where did you get such a thing?" Tristan kept the cannon pointed at him.

"Just hand it over. It's far more dangerous than you could imagine."

"I'm not as sheltered as you may have been led to believe." Tristan sighted along the barrel directly at the center of Dominick's chest, dropping low behind the overturned table. "I've been out there in the real world. Even before that, my tutors were never all that skilled at keeping me focused only on the things they were commissioned to teach me. Now, this little thing could, depending on what you loaded it with, destroy this police station. It could possibly, if you loaded it right, have enough detonation power to kill most of the people here on New Brooklyn. It might, if you knew what you were doing, be able to throw an explosive charge all the way up to a transport hovering over a shuttle port on Hamshire. You did say you work for Uncle Leblanc, right? So does he know you have this? Did he maybe give it to you?"

Tristan saw a flinch in Dominick's eyes that told him he'd hit home. He'd found the idiot responsible for all those deaths. He was so tempted to just pull the trigger and be done with it. There wouldn't be enough left to send home. It was tempting but dangerous. Likely there wouldn't be enough of either of them to identify.

Dominick sidled to the right. Tristan followed him with the cannon.

"This is a bit ridiculous, sire."

"You're the one who brought this weapon into the station." Tristan forced himself to hold the cannon as steady as possible. *Please be smart; back down.*

"You have no idea what one can do in the name of the royal family if you have the right connections. And you, sire, don't have those connections anymore. Your little joke on the people of this nation is over. You died, according to all official records, months ago in a terrorist attack. And that's the way it's going to stay. Someone is going to be arrested for impersonating you and hoaxing the citizens of the kingdom, and within a few months, it will be over. You'll be gone and Princess Aramelia will be the heir, crowned and everything."

"Have you checked with her? Does she even want the job? I mean, if anyone had asked me, I would have turned them down. It's a shit job, even with all the perks. If I hadn't been born to it, I would have been sorry for the poor slob who had to take it on." *Don't make me use it. Please don't make me use it.*

"You're a very unusual boy. Anyone else would be thrilled to be in your position."

"Not right now. Stop moving."

Dominick held up his hands and stopped moving. "Well, of course not. I meant before you died."

"Even then, anyone smart enough to do the job would be smart enough to realize it's all work and no play." Tristan shifted the table so it was perfectly between them again.

"You seem to think you're smart." Dominick had his own weapon pointed at Tristan.

"I was smart enough to avoid your last assassination attempt."

#

Murphy sat on his bench, letting his tears flow freely. There was no one to mock him for crying and really no other reason to keep it in check. Sure, it would be caught on vid, but if anyone thought it was funny enough to hack and put out there, he'd welcome the publicity at this point. Watching Tristan get taken away was like a slap in the face. A reminder that he was nothing more than an ungraduated teenager out on a wild adventure and only playing at being a big shot. He'd found the princess and she hated him for it. Yeah! No one was going to believe him anyway. They were both locked up without even knowing why. The adventure was over. With any luck, he'd get a chance to call his parents before they did anything permanent.

It was hard to tell time in a cell. His body didn't keep time the way a clock did. It was highly suggestive. If he tried to track time by how often he needed to pee, then he would need to pee every five minutes. The only thing that kept his mind off his ultimate failure that his life had become was to sleep.

The cell made even that difficult. The bench was hard and unyielding. There was nothing to put his head on. The lights were daylight-bright all the time, and he was left with only his thoughts for company. Some unknown time later, when his tears had dried into crusty streaks on his cheeks, the guards returned. This time there were five of them. He didn't even bother to see if he recognized any of them from before.

They opened Emalynn's cell first, but before dragging her off to an unknown fate, they opened his as well. He let them haul him to his feet but twisted out of their grips and lay back down before they could drag him from the cell. They grabbed him again, this time tighter.

"Where are you taking us? Why are we being held?"

He didn't really expect an answer this time any more than any other time since they'd locked them in. He wasn't disappointed. Emalynn wouldn't look at him. She didn't fight when they pushed her out the door and down the stark corridor through which they'd entered.

"Ly." Murphy tried to get her attention. "Ly, it's not over yet."

She didn't give any hint that she heard him.

They took a turn Murphy hadn't noticed on his way in. The new corridor looked exactly the same as the other one—stark-white walls, shadowless lighting, and absolutely no decoration beyond door numbers on the infrequent doors. They passed three doors labeled "interview room" until they were pushed through a fourth identical doorway.

The room on the other side was a stark all-white conference room divided into two by a clear wall. On this side there was half a conference table and three chairs. There was no handle on the inside of the door and no controls of any kind on the walls. On the other side was the other half of the conference table, five black office chairs on wheels, and the two people he was both happy and upset to see. His parents were sitting in the office chairs, while three others he didn't recognize immediately stood behind them.

The guards left them, locking them into their half of the room. Murphy fought the urge to turn and bang on the door, screaming that he'd rather spend the rest of his life in the holding cell.

"Murphy." His mother greeted him, standing up. "It's good to see you."

Her voice was strained, as though she'd been crying or yelling. It wasn't the first time they'd had conversations through a safety wall in a police station.

"And this must be the... Emalynn?" Father waved to Emalynn.

She didn't move. Not so much as a single muscle flexed or relaxed. She just stood where she'd stopped, arms limp at her sides, head bowed, and eyes just barely open.

"Please sit down, both of you." Mother waved at the chairs. "We have so much to talk about and only a little time."

Murphy sat in the chair closest to Father. Emalynn remained where she was.

"Ly, please sit." Murphy kept his voice soft. He'd seen what she could do when she calculated her fight. He didn't want to know what would happen if she let loose with pure emotion.

There was an awkward silence while everyone waited for someone else to break the tension. Murphy turned to look at the table, then forced himself to remain still. Mother fidgeted with the edge of the tabletop, her eyes darting around the room. Father, though, kept his eyes on Emalynn.

"We heard you were here and came to take you home. We didn't expect to find you in jail." Father's misplaced joke fell flat.

"You shouldn't have come," Murphy said. "Didn't Davy tell you?"

"Davy told us you'd found, um, her." Mom glanced at

Emalynn. "But he also said you were straying from the plan. We couldn't just let all our work go to waste."

"What work, Mom? The plan expired years ago. It's too late to raise her with our values. Be happy she's still alive and was raised as a commoner." He watched Emalynn out of the corner of his eye.

"Murphy." Dad used that fatherly tone that used to mean big trouble. Today it showed how scared he was to be out of control.

"Dad." Murphy tried to reflect the same tone. "I'm not a little boy anymore. I've been out there trying to save your precious plan, but she grew up with a good mother and a view on all the things your plan was about. It's time for you to trust me."

That little speech earned him glares from both parents and the three standing behind them. Why hadn't he seen it before? His parents were every bit as royal as Tristan's. They didn't have the recognized bloodline or the riches, but in their own circles, they commanded just as much power and loyalty. If he thought about it, he, too, had privileges others didn't get. They weren't the same, but they set him apart just as much. The thought made him want to lose his lunch.

"It's Emalynn, right?" Mom turned her attention away from Murphy. "We've come to get you out of this—"

"I know why you came." Emalynn cut her off.

"Good. Let me introduce myself—"

"Don't bother."

Murphy didn't know whether to cheer or duck for cover. The glares he'd received were nothing compared to the eye daggers aimed at Emalynn. Emalynn had finally raised her eyes from the floor and was glaring daggers just as sharp back at Mom.

"I know who you are, Caroline and Grady Sanchain. You're the ones who planned for me to be kidnapped. You're the ones who stole my life. You're the idiots who couldn't finish the job and left me with a mercenary for a mother. You're the ones who didn't search hard enough all these years. Do you know what she had to do to keep me safe and fed and educated, all in the hopes that you would complete your contract someday? She became a smuggler. When that wasn't enough anymore, she turned to assassinations. That's right. Your precious princess was raised by an assassin. But from what I've seen since her murder, it was the better option for me. Now you think just because you had a plan, I'm just going to walk over there and hug you like my long-lost mother? You're even more stupid than Murphy's glowing praise led me to believe. I'm not going anywhere with you."

The deadly silence that coated the room after that was almost comforting. Now it was his parents' turn to stare at the floor, for a brief moment. Then Murphy saw the hardening of his mother's expression.

"You aren't going to have a choice. You are a minor in possession of stolen property. They will turn you over to my custody as your legal guardian."

Don't be that stupid, Mom. Murphy pleaded in his mind. *You don't know what she can do.*

"No."

That word filled Murphy with absolute dread.

CHAPTER EIGHTEEN

EMALYNN - POLICE CUSTODY

"I think you don't understand." Mrs. Sanchain had taken on that mother tone that never worked with any child over the age of ten.

"I think *you* aren't listening." Emalynn echoed the same tone. "I told you I don't want to have anything to do with an organization that would kidnap a child. You weren't there when I needed a mother. You didn't fulfill your contract with Baba. What makes you think I'm going to trust you?"

"Ly..." Murphy pleaded.

"Enough out of you too." She turned to glare at him. "You are her son through and through." She took a step toward him and he scampered away. "Did you really think I would love you, trust you, for hiding my past from me?"

Murphy squeaked. He put the heavy metal conference table between them. "Ly, calm down."

"No." She lunged at him, making everyone jump.

"Emalynn..." Mrs. Sanchain started.

Tristan's fear flooded through their connection. She saw, like in a dream, the mini cannon. She flipped the table onto its side and ducked. She had just enough time to think Murphy was in danger before the wall exploded. There was smoke and shrapnel everywhere. Emalynn watched in horror as Murphy flew back against the wall, changing from his usual dark color to a bright red. Emalynn saw Baba and Murphy lying on the ground in front of her, their bodies mangled beyond recognition. The smell of expended explosives and blood filled the room as the table pushed her through the wall too.

"No!" She screamed, but there was no sound. "No!"

She tried to reach for him. If she could just catch him

before he finished landing, maybe she could save him. Maybe she could hold him and that would be enough. It wouldn't happen.

She shoved the smashed table off of her and tried to stand, but her right knee wouldn't hold her. It was a bloody mess. She ripped off the leg of her pants to get a better look. It was swollen and bloody. Everything was bloody and covered in dust. She tied the tatters of her pants around her knee to brace it before stumbling out to find Murphy.

She found a length of pipe just long enough to be a cane and heavy enough to make her feel armed. Then she found Murphy. What was left of him. He was sprawled at too many angles, with blood congealing all around him. There were many shards of wall and glass penetrating deep into his body. A metal strut poked through his ribs, keeping him from the floor.

"Oh, Murphy," she whispered, though her voice was swallowed in the echoes of the explosion. "I'm so sorry. I didn't mean it. I didn't mean to do any of this." Tears flowed down her cheeks, but there was no time to mourn.

Emalynn looked around at the destruction. The glass wall that separated her from the Alecti Army was gone. Most of its shards were in their side of the room. The white walls on that side were just as spattered in red as they were on her side. She hobbled over to find that all five of them were as mangled as Murphy. With her luck, if anyone found her here, she was going to be blamed for this mess. She was in enough trouble and debt without having to rebuild a shuttle port.

She needed to find the source of the explosion. She needed to find Tristan. The room on the other side of the missing wall had been a little smaller than this one. There were bloodstains all over the walls and the overturned table there too. The far wall was mostly a hole, with the furniture all smashed up against the far wall in the room beyond that.

Emalynn picked her way across the mess. She found a shoe sitting in the middle of an otherwise empty area just beyond the wall. Her stomach turned at the thought that it might have been Tristan's until she realized it wasn't even his size. This was a high-end fashion shoe that was more about looks than comfort. Tristan had been wearing athletic shoes. It wasn't him. She dropped the shoe and looked for any signs of a survivor in this room.

The conference table was flipped and driven into the wall the same way hers was. She picked her way through the debris as quietly as she could, knowing that anyone else near the blast zone was going to be just as deaf as she was. But how quick would rescue workers get here? She needed to find Tristan and get out before anyone even knew they were here.

Tristan looked almost dead under all the blood and gore behind the table. She pulled off her jacket and used it to clean off most of the blood. There was a gash on his head and another on his arm, but they had already stopped bleeding. She couldn't see any obvious broken bones. With her own injuries, it would be impossible to carry him safely. She found a sheet of wall just about big enough to strap him to so she could drag him out with her.

She was still trying to pull wires out of the wreckage when the rescue workers arrived—four strong-looking women with medical kits and a backboard. Emalynn knocked the first one back when they startled her.

"He's my brother. Please help him."

They said something to her, but the ringing from the blast was too loud.

"I can't hear." She pointed at her ears.

They nodded, set down their kits, and made soothing gestures. Emalynn tried not to scowl at them. She wasn't stupid, just deaf. One EMT stayed with Emalynn, first getting her ears back to normal, then working on her knee.

"What happened in here?"

"Someone tried to kill him."

"What? Why?" The woman looked over to where the other three were working to get Tristan onto the backboard. Emalynn took the opportunity to steal the woman's stunner.

"I don't know, but it's not the first attempt." Emalynn looked around as though paranoid. "We thought being in jail would be safe."

"Yeah," the woman agreed. "It should be." She finished binding Emalynn's knee. "Now let's see if you can stand on that."

It still hurt, but not as much. She could put some weight on it but would still need help walking. That would make things a little easier. One of them was going to have to help her, leaving two to carry Tristan and one to haul all the rest of the stuff.

"How is he?"

"Not dead," one of the women called back.

"What happens now?" Emalynn let her voice tremble.

"We finish stabilizing your injuries and his. Then we'll get you out to ambulance for a quick trip to the hospital," said the one who was treating her.

Emalynn nodded and let them finish their work. They passed another team coming in, and the one woman who was carrying all the supplies joined them to look for more survivors. They passed three more teams of rescue workers and several cops in various uniforms. The EMTs fended them off with practiced skill. Emalynn could see barricade for the reporters too. She tried to keep her face hidden but was sure they would be spotted. She let them load her into the ambulance and drive away from the scene before pressing the stunner into the side of the EMT who had helped her.

"Don't go to the hospital. It's not safe."

"What are you doing?" The driver didn't flinch—more credit to her.

"Taking control." Emalynn lifted the stunner so the others could see it in the rearview mirror. "If a police station isn't safe enough, I'm not going to trust a hospital. Get me to my shuttle."

"You're crazy," the third EMT said, reaching for her own stunner. Emalynn held that one up too.

"I know how to use these, but I don't want to."

"Right." The driver shifted lanes and headed toward the shuttle port. "Should I call ahead?"

"No. We don't know who's trying to kill us, so the less they know the better."

"What if it was us?"

"I'd have to kill you."

They rode in silence until they joined the queue for the shuttle port.

"What's the name of your shuttle?" The driver waved off a question from the other EMT.

"Why?"

"We're going to have to tell them something at the gate. And it will help them get ready fast enough to keep you safe."

"You believe me?"

"It doesn't matter. I'm going to help you."

At the gate, the driver gave a wonderful line to the guard about how critical it was to get that shuttle ready and cleared for takeoff immediately. She didn't let the guard give her any hang-ups. They expected to meet the shuttle on the tarmac, and yes, it was life-critical.

Everything was ready when the ambulance pulled up. They loaded Tristan onto shuttle with haste and helped Emalynn with exaggerated care for the benefit of the shuttle security who were standing there. Inside, the driver gave Emalynn a quick lesson in how to care for Tristan.

"Now, give us back our stunners."

Emalynn hesitated.

"You don't want the charges of stealing our stunners. Give them back and we can say you had a convincing argument."

"Why would you do that for me?" She wanted to keep them, as a feeling of safety, but the EMT was right. And they wouldn't do her any good on the shuttle anyway.

"Call it a goodwill gesture. Just get out of my city." She held out her hands for the stunners.

Emalynn handed them over. She watched the EMTs exit the shuttle before turning to her control panel and getting ready to launch. The tower gave her the all clear and she launched as soon as the little shuttle was ready. She didn't breathe until she was in orbit.

#

TRISTAN – LONG-RANGE SHUTTLE

Tristan felt the cold, flat surface below him before he opened his eyes. He was alive. Or death hurt a lot more than he'd imagined. He opened his eyes to the ceiling of the shuttle. He tried to roll over and whimpered in pain.

"No, don't move." Emalynn slid into view. Her eyes were lined with dark circles and her cheeks covered in lace-like cuts. There were bandages covering most of her arms. "You were hit pretty hard. I thought I'd lost you..."

He tried to think through the pain in his head. He thought there was something off about what she'd said, but it was gone before he could catch it.

"How did you get out? How did you find me?"

"We... I was in the next room when the bomb went off. There was no wall between us when the dust settled. Everyone was so concerned about the explosion that they didn't stop me from taking you or the shuttle."

"Was Murphy there too?" He regretted the question as soon as it was past his lips.

Tears flowed in great torrents down her cheeks. She nodded weakly. He tried to reach up to help wipe away the tears. His hand was bound in a thick cast. She caught it and pushed it back down to his side.

"Murphy... He..." She took more time to swallow the pain

enough to tell him. "He caught the blast head on." She shook her head.

"I'm sorry." His own tears clouded his eyes.

"It's not your fault." She wiped his tears away.

"It is my fault." He could feel his own throat tighten up, making his voice squeak.

"You weren't the one trying to kill us. You weren't the coward who planted the bomb." She got a severe look in her eyes that scared him.

He nodded, willing his voice to work. "I did."

"What?"

"The bomb. I set the bomb." The sobs took him then. He wanted to explain, but there were no words.

"It's still not your fault." She didn't look at him when she said it. "You need to eat something. It's been days and I didn't have an IV for you."

She disappeared somewhere over his head. Tristan tried to sit up again, this time rolling in the other direction. That hurt just as much. He lay back down, trying to feel anything that didn't hurt. How had he managed to survive at all?

"Here, I have a simple soup." She sat by his head with her legs crossed. She lifted his shoulders until she could scoot her legs under them and support his head on her stomach. "I don't have anything better to hold you up. Tell me if it's too hot."

A spoon appeared in front of him.

"This is ridiculous." He tried to move away from her but found only pain in every direction.

"Hold still and open your mouth."

"I can feed myself."

"Not at the moment. You don't have working hands."

How embarrassing. Then his stomach decided to voice its opinion about the food, which smelled really good. He gave in and opened his mouth. The flavors that came through were everything the scent had promised. He almost hated to swallow because then the flavor would be gone.

"Where did you get that?"

"I made it." She held another spoonful for him.

He savored and swallowed. "With what?"

"The supplies Mav gave us. They sent their best herbs."

She shoved the spoon into his mouth, preventing further conversation. Three more spoonfuls ushered him into the blackness of sleep.

The next time he woke, he almost made it to a sitting

position before Emalynn brought the soup. "Where are we?"

"Drifting cold." She pushed a spoonful of the soup into his mouth. The flavors helped distract him from everything else.

His dreams were filled with horrible images of things blowing up or falling apart. The next time he woke, he was heavier. The pain of just lying still was more than he could handle and he didn't fight the sleep after each bit of soup she fed him.

Eventually, the pain subsided and he was able to roll up to a seated position. The casts around his arms were replaced with smaller versions, giving him some flexibility in his fingers. He managed to get into the copilot's chair on his own. That's when he noticed the Other ship in the lower edge of the front view screen.

"Where are we going?"

"Home," she said. "I think."

"Home? As in Prime? I didn't think Others ever went to Prime."

She shrugged. "Are you hungry?"

He didn't want to change the subject, but his stomach answered for him. "Is there something I can feed myself?"

"Can you move your fingers?"

He held up his hand and wiggled his fingers. They didn't give much movement, but he was able to touch each to his thumb when she asked him to.

"We have some apples I can cut up for you and a nutrition bar." She listed several other things as she walked to the back.

The star charts showed they were in Ashtile County. They might really be headed for Prime. The scans also showed crowds of ships in the area. More than he would expect, even this close to the center of the human worlds.

Emalynn returned with the promised food, all cut up into bite-sized pieces.

"How did you find an Other coming here?" Tristan asked as she eased into her seat.

"I'm not sure. I was doing my best to evade the pursuit from New Brooklyn when I caught her signal. She showed me where she was, so I set a course and drifted cold for a couple of days."

Tristan looked at her. "Others don't contact us."

"This one did." She shrugged. "Actually, she came to find me."

"And you trusted her?"

"More than any human right now."

He agreed. Maybe they would be better off going to live with the Others and leaving humanity behind. "What are we going to do?"

"I'm tired of running." She stared out the view screen. "Lord Leblanc has made his move. Those ships out there aren't what they say they are. Look." The display zoomed in on a cluster of small passenger ships and cargo vessels. These ships were sleek, with no extra space for passengers or holds full of cargo. They bristled with ports and maneuvering thrusters.

Tristan swallowed hard. The royal line had been unbroken since the beginning. He couldn't be the one to break it. He was not going to let his uncle force his way into power.

"What's the plan?"

Emalynn fiddled with the controls in front of her. "Getting to Prime will be easy. No one will see us on the Others' ship. After that, um, code 58?"

"I don't really want to get arrested again," Tristan said.

"Maybe we can skip that step."

Code 58 was supposed to get you a chance to tell your story and have it verified. If they were still on the Other ship, they might be able to use it to get a remote audience with the queen. Would that be enough? Had anything they'd done been enough? For all they knew, this had been part of Lord Leblanc's plan from the beginning. Or maybe the succession hadn't gone his way. It might be that their parents knew what was going on already.

"Do you know if our video made it out?" he asked.

"Yes. It got out to the gossip sites but was silenced about a day later."

"Then we might have a chance to get a vid call through. How do we explain the Others' ship?"

She just shook her head. "Really, with everything else we're going to be showing them, I think the Others will be only a minor detail."

CHAPTER NINETEEN

EMALYNN – LONG-RANGE SHUTTLE

Emalynn put a little extra effort into making herself look good when she woke up. They were just an hour from falling into orbit around Prime.

She hoped the Other understood and believed when she told her to take a high orbit. She didn't know how to explain that this planet was more heavily armed than any of the other human worlds and would be far more offended at having an Others' ship take orbit. She wasn't even sure how she'd managed to get her to bring them to Prime.

She set a transmission to send the number 58 in as many formats as she could think of. She hoped it would be seen as coming from the Others' ship. She was surprised to find that the Other had picked up and copied the transmission, adding a few formats Emalynn couldn't understand.

She checked on Tristan before heading to the pilot's seat. He'd been sleeping so much and eating so little, he was beginning to look too thin. He needed to get to a hospital. A polite text to Lord Leblanc and whoever else was trying to take down the government wasn't going to make that possible.

A ping on the main screen called her to the pilot's chair. It was the Other pilot, arms in the question position, overlaid by an orbit diagram that would keep them well above all other ships and stations in orbit. Emalynn acknowledged with the yes sign. She added a diagram she hoped looked like transmissions that continued. The Other gave her the yes sign before closing the connection. The transmissions continued, so it must have worked.

She barely had time to look back at Tristan when the Other was back on her screen, arms in the question position. A small image in the lower left showed a formal-looking woman in a royal uniform. Emalynn focused on the image, bringing it larger in her screen and allowing the sound to transmit as well.

"Unknown transport, please state your identity and the nature of your inquiry." The woman used a strange accent, then repeated the statement in a different accent.

"Tristan, wake up." She reached over to nudge him.

"Hmm." He shifted about.

"We're there, and I need you."

That brought his eyes open. She could see the moment he understood what was on the screen as he sat up, looking fully awake.

"What have you told them?"

"Nothing yet. That's being sent through the Other." She reopened the view of the Other pilot. "What should I tell them? About us or the coup?"

"They probably know about the coup. Tell them about us."

Emalynn pulled up a picture of the two of them together that they'd never released during the gossip campaign. Then she brought up the diagram of the planet with their orbit. She made a small copy of the picture and showed it moving from their little dot to the planet.

"If that works, we should get their attention."

The Other pilot acknowledged with the yes gesture but didn't close the connection.

"What the hell?" the woman said and turned to call another woman into the screen. "Are they saying that they have those kids?"

"Oh, holy…" the new woman said. "That's Tristan. Get the commander down here now!" She turned to the transmission, speaking directly into the camera. "I don't know who you are, but you will have to prove that you have those children alive and well or be prepared to defend yourself."

Emalynn opened a new window, a live feed from the shuttle communications system. She sent it to the Other ship. The longer they kept the Other involved, the longer before unwanted people would figure out what was going on. She told the Other to transmit this the same way she had the pictures.

Emalynn waited for a count of thirty. "We are fine."

"Oh dear lords, what happened to them?" The women were joined by several others leaning over their chairs.

The Other came on with the question sign. Emalynn gave a diagram with bits bouncing back and forth. She highlighted the planet and gave the question sign, then highlighted the Other and gave the yes sign. The Other pilot gave the yes sign and shook a little. Emalynn decided that must have been a laugh. Now the Other pilot shifted a little and gave the yes sign to the women on the other screen.

"Is she trying to talk to them?" Tristan asked quietly.

"I think so."

"But they don't know how."

Emalynn shrugged.

"I don't understand what is going on," one woman said. "They have those kids."

A woman in a commander's uniform came to the center of the transmission. "Where are the children?" the commander demanded of the Other.

Emalynn sent a diagram showing the planet in red and the Other ship with orbit in blue with a small red dot on the Other dot.

The Other pilot gave the question sign. Emalynn made her own image fade out. Make the commander learn to be creative and maybe this would work out. Tristan looked his own question at her.

"Even if they don't believe us about being the prince and princess, we've just made ourselves more valuable than any other teens in the universe," she explained.

"But you're teaching them your skills. We won't be valuable for long."

"We will if they think we know more."

"Do we?" he asked.

"No, but they don't need to know that."

Tristan shook his head. They watched the scene in the communications room as the women tried to figure out what they were seeing.

"We need to talk to the children directly."

Emalynn showed what the commander had said as best she could. The Other questioned. "Yes," Emalynn said.

She could see the quality change when the connection became direct, though the Other pilot stayed connected as well. Emalynn acknowledged her before turning to talk to the commander.

"I am Emalynn and this is my brother Tristan. We want to talk to our parents."

"Who are your parents? No, what are you doing on an Other ship?"

Emalynn laughed a little. Which bit should she answer first?

"King Levon and Queen Treylyn of the house of Tharlin."

"We'll have to check out your claim. You do know that."

"Yes," Emalynn said. "Can you do that without taking us into custody? We've had some bad experiences." She waved at the scars that were still red on her cheeks.

There was a murmured discussion among all the women. The only thing Emalynn heard clearly was that they didn't know how to take them into custody.

"We'll see about that. Where is your ship?"

"On the Others' ship." Their scans should have showed them that by now.

The sensors told her they were being scanned with a wide range of frequencies.

"How did you get there?"

Emalynn smiled. "We asked for a ride and she agreed."

There was a pause while the commander digested that. "Explain that a bit more."

"There's not much more to it. I sent out a request for a ride like this." She sent a copy of the message she'd sent when she left New Brooklyn. "This ship responded. I used these diagrams to tell her where we wanted to go, and she agreed. Here we are. She's worried about the number of ships circling this system."

Tristan smiled at her subtly.

"Do you have any idea of the risk you've taken? You could have started a war with the Others."

"Tell that to all the smugglers who've been hitching rides for generations. I'm more concerned about the warships actually."

"Commander, do you think we are in danger of war when there is only a single ship here?" Tristan put in. "The war you need to watch out for is the one that was started when my transport was destroyed."

The commander paused again. "I still need to verify your identities."

Emalynn smiled. "How would you like to do that?"

"The easiest way would be to check your identity chits."

"Not really," Tristan said. "Mine's been altered and hers was never part of the royal database."

"All the more reason to doubt you."

Emalynn couldn't argue that point. "Well, we only wish to

speak with our parents. You can verify that we are safe at least, I assume."

The commander scowled. "Your point."

"We're happy to stay right where we are until we get the chance to talk to them. All we're asking of you is to take our request to them. What danger can that pose?" Emalynn tried to look as innocent as she could, even though this woman was driving her nuts.

"Also, we have delivered information about a threat under code 58," Tristan said. "I would hope you would look into that as well, though we expect no report on what you find."

There was a long pause while the commander talked to the people around her. Emalynn cut their mics as well.

"Are you sure about all this?" Tristan asked.

"No." Emalynn admitted.

"What if they don't talk to us?"

"I don't know."

The commander came on again. "You are approved only for the orbit you are in. Any change from that and you will be considered an enemy of the state. Do you understand?"

"Yes," Emalynn said. The signal went dead. Emalynn could see the Other pilot in the question position. She pulled up the diagram of the orbit again. She added a couple of tangents with red X's through them.

The Other pilot highlighted one of the tangents and sent a picture of an explosion with her arms in the question position. Emalynn responded with yes. The pilot acknowledged and cut the connection.

"Now we wait?" Tristan asked.

Emalynn nodded, but her attention was on a proximity reading that had been blocked by the conversation.

"Oh no. We were followed."

"Oh shit."

They were still far out and hard to identify, but the recorded trajectory showed that it had been in one of the militia encampments they'd passed by.

"Did they hear all that?" Tristan asked.

"I doubt it matters."

If they did anything preemptively, they'd lose credibility. If they waited, they could be dead with a cross-species incident as their legacy before they got a chance to do anything. Emalynn dropped her head to the console.

#

Tristan stared at the image the sensors were able to put up. It wasn't enough to tell what kind of ship it was. He'd already enhanced the sensors as much as he was able. Damn it. They might not be in a dungeon, but they were trapped all the same.

"We need to tell the Other pilot about that ship," Tristan said.

"Yeah." Emalynn agreed. "But what if they decide to do something stupid?"

The Other pilot contacted with a picture of the ship and her arms in the horizontal position. Her image was much clearer. It showed that the ship was a fighter class with the weapons fully mounted.

"Shit," Tristan muttered. There was a crest on the side of the ship, not quite visible. "Can she highlight that crest?" He pointed to it.

Emalynn made a red circle around the crest and put her arms in the horizontal position.

"That's how you ask a question?" He mimicked the gesture.

She nodded.

He had the arm gestures down then: up for yes, cross for no, horizontal for question. The rest he was still trying to figure out. How did Emalynn know what to do with all the images and symbols she used?

The Other pilot made that part of the image bigger. The angle was still bad, but it was clear enough for Tristan to recognize the coat of arms.

"That ship belongs to Lord Leblanc."

"He's not going to care about starting a war with the Others, is he?" She was already letting her fingers dance over the controls.

"Not from what I've seen of him."

She nodded and continued working. The blue dot that was them was enclosed in a green circle. Then a red dot moved toward the circle and bounced away. She played this sequence for the Other. The Other took her time in responding. Then the sequence came back first as Emalynn had offered and the second time with the red dot simply stopping. She displayed the question sign.

Emalynn added more green circles and more red dots, showing some stopping farther out from the blue dot. The Other

176

held her arms in the no position until the red dot passed the farthest circle, then shifted to yes until the red dot passed the second to innermost circle, when she shifted back to no.

Emalynn faded the green circle farthest out and the three closer in, leaving two green circles. Then she added more red dots all coming toward them and all stopping between the two green circles. The Other replayed with her arms in the yes position.

"What's all that?" Tristan asked.

"She can block him if he gets too close. I think. I can't tell scale so I don't know what that means." She shrugged. "It's something."

"I just hope it's out of weapons range."

"Or she can deal with those too. I don't know how to ask for that."

Tristan stared at the scene before them. So many possibilities. "Can you tell her that ships with that crest are dangers to us? Maybe she can help."

"I'll try." Her fingers flew across the keypad. The images were more confusing than helpful, and he had to look away. He took the time to start sorting through the images they had of the ships around them. There were all manner of civilian ships around and any one of them could be harboring the enemy.

"She can help," Emalynn announced. "We're going to make it through this alive, I think."

Tristan let out a sigh. "Now we have to explain which ships are the bad guys."

"What? No. She needs to stay out of our war." Emalynn gave him a distressed look. "We don't want the Others involved."

"She's already involved. She got involved when she picked us up. Now she needs to know what's going on. That ship out there, Lord Leblanc, isn't going to care that she's supposed to be neutral."

Emalynn turned away from him. He wished they could protect the Other too. He opened his mouth to say something, but the com interrupted. The screen lit up with an image of the king in his most regal appearance, gold crown and all.

"This had better be important."

"Father." Tristan stared at the screen. He'd never been so thrilled to see that man in his life.

"Who are you?" The severity of his tone didn't match the light in his eyes.

"I'm your son, Tristan, prince and heir to the house of

Tharlin."

"Impossible. My son was killed in an attack two months ago."

"I wasn't on the transport. Techani Kenchi and I were at the mall, off schedule. I wanted a chance to be a real teenager."

The king's eyes shifted to the left where Emalynn was staring up at the overlarge image of the king's face. "Who are you?"

"My name is Emalynn. I think I may be Tristan's twin."

"I don't have time for fantasies."

"Then don't worry about that now." Emalynn looked directly at the king through the screen. "Go with what you know. Someone tried to kill your son. We know who that was and why. Are you going to believe us or are we speaking into the wind?"

Tristan winced at the forward attitude she took.

"Why should I believe you? So far all you've done is spout fantasies about talking with the Others and being my kin. What proof do you have?"

"Father..."

"Don't call me that."

"Sire." Emalynn commanded his attention again. Tristan was impressed with how much she sounded just like him. "Your experts should be able to tell you how our little shuttle managed to get into orbit around Prime. That's not us spouting fantasies. You can believe what you like about all the rest, but you can't dispute the fact that we are right now sitting on the back of an Others' ship. And if you choose not to believe us, then you'll get all the proof you need in about..." She paused to check the readings. "Ten minutes when Lord Leblanc's ship gets in range and starts shooting at us. When that happens, he'll also be shooting at an Others' ship. I don't think you want to deal with that kind of incident. We've never really seen what kind of weapons the Others carry. We've never had reason to dispute with them. Don't let something as silly as this be a reason to change that."

The king glared at Emalynn for having the gall to speak to him like that. Tristan had never realized how petty his father could be over silly things like protocol.

"You have proof of this?"

"Yes, sire," Emalynn said, "but not time to show you. Lord Leblanc has a fighter coming in now. Is it too much to ask for guards to protect this emissary of the Others? She had her own reasons for coming here."

178

Emalynn overlaid the image they'd received from the Other pilot of the ship that was approaching them. Tristan knew such insolence was going to make their case even harder to get through. He could only hope his father was more interested in the facts and the hope that his son was alive than his pride.

"Sire," Tristan nearly choked on the word. "As you can see here, this is the crest of Leblanc." Tristan added a bit of highlight to the image. "You can also see in this image that the weapons banks are fully deployed and ready to fire. Emalynn, can you call up the images of the militias?"

She did without arguing with him.

"These are scans we took ourselves as we were passing through the Delta system. We'd heard rumors that militias were gathering around Prime. We don't know if they have any connection to Lord Leblanc, but we thought you might like to know they are there."

Something beeped on the control panel.

"There are more guard ships surrounding us. They have their weapons charged." Emalynn looked up at the screen. "Excuse me, sire, but in the interest of not causing an interspecies disaster, I think I should explain to our host and guest what is happening. What would you like me to tell her?"

The king looked even grumpier than before. "Tell her to trust us to keep order in our own house. And ask what she is here for."

"Yes, sire, and thank you for your protection."

She cut the link with the king, another mistake that was going to cost them. The Other pilot was already trying to call them. Tristan watched with awe as she made the images dance across the screen the way her fingers danced on the controls. The ease of communication, if you could call it that, amazed Tristan. Years of research by experts had shown no progress.

It all ended with signs of agreement on both sides.

"Do you think we should call the king back to tell him she wants to talk to him?" Emalynn asked when the screen went dead.

"Considering how many protocols we mashed in our last contact, I think we'd better wait until all this is over."

"What?"

"By his standards, we were rude."

"You've got to be kidding."

Tristan could only shrug.

CHAPTER TWENTY

EMALYNN – PRIME ORBIT

Great, Emalynn thought, *just great.* She had just ruined their last chance to be taken seriously by the royals, which meant Prince Tristan would stay dead and she'd stay an orphan. Worse than that, they were now enemies of the state.

Emalynn shifted the view on the main screen and called up all their stats on the shuttle. Not surprising, they were doing very well on life support, plenty of oxygen and water. They even had full batteries for the minimal defense systems on the shuttle. They were tied into the local network on Prime for all of their data needs. She changed the screen again and this time called up the data on all the ships they could see—transports and shippers, even a couple of luxury cruisers in this direction. The same when she shifted to another view.

"What are you looking for?" Tristan blocked her next attempt to change the main screen.

"I don't know."

"Look, just relax a bit. There's nothing more we can do right now."

Emalynn opened her mouth to tell him to shut his. Instead, she skirted his block and changed the view again, to yet another set of civilian ships going about their regular business, completely unaware of the war they were about to get into.

"I need to do something."

"Like what?"

"Like warn them." She waved at the luxury liner that was dominating this view. "They have no idea what's about to happen."

Tristan looked up at the screen with more scrutiny than it warranted. "Maybe they do." The view narrowed onto the luxury liner.

It didn't look like any luxury liner she'd ever seen. There were very few view ports, and the ones they could see were tiny. The gray paint showed more scratches than the worst cargo vessel she'd ever smuggled on. Where the observation decks should have been, there were cannons.

"That's not a luxury liner." Emalynn narrowed the focus farther and could pick out shield generators nestled among the reinforced body plates. "How can they...?" She knew the trick of changing a ship's ID tag. Though she'd never seen a smuggler change anything more than the name of a ship, she knew it was possible.

"How many more are there?"

They split the screen and scanned all the nearest vessels. Most of the ships were exactly what their IDs said they were. Too many were weaponized. Everything from small in-system shuttles to cargo drones were armed with percussive and energy cannons.

"They outnumber the royal and planetary defenses combined." Tristan had compiled a list of all the ships they'd found in their limited view of the system.

"We have to do something." Emalynn pulled up all the access they could get. She could see the royal network that the king had used. "We have to tell them."

"We can't."

Emalynn gave him her best "shut it" look and went on looking for an open media portal.

"We are under a code 58. If we do anything, we will lose any chance of being believed."

"They told us not to change orbit. They never said we shouldn't tell them if we find more relevant information. And really, does it matter that we followed the rules if your uncle wins?"

Tristan opened his mouth but closed it tight without saying anything. Emalynn went back to seeking something she could use to alert the royal forces that they were in for a bigger fight. She found an untended broadcast channel. She had almost secured the channel when she realized she didn't know what to say.

"How do we get their attention?" Tristan asked. He had the video editor open on his side of the screen.

"How did you get that on the shuttle com?" Emalynn asked.

182

He shrugged. "I just downloaded it. It took some configuring to get it to sit right. I'm not sure it's fully functional. But it should do what we need it to."

Of course. "We just have to be us." Emalynn could see it now. When they thought they were pulling off their big plan, they were just setting the stage for this.

It took only a few minutes to get everything set and ready. In that time, the weaponized ships had begun to move into a screen around the planet, evenly spaced in a high orbit. The real civilian ships were in lower orbits.

"Let's do this."

Tristan nodded and started the recording. Emalynn connected with the open channel, supplanting the broadcast there.

"Hi there, all you Tristan hunters." Tristan started. "We want to thank you for all your participation. You've done a wonderful job."

"Now there is just one thing left to complete the game." Emalynn picked up. "The last step to bringing Prince Tristan back and revealing the final secret."

"Somewhere on one of these ships, currently in orbit around Prime, is the key." Tristan sent the links to all the weaponized ships.

"All you have to do is be the first to find it." Emalynn started a cascade of all the close-up images they had with the weapons ports showing and their civilian IDs. "Find the real ship among all of these. I'll give you a hint. Disrupting the fake ones will make it easier."

"Thank you once again for all your participation. We look forward to the competition."

They cut the broadcast just in time to see the first strikes of the battle. It was hard to watch at first as the enemy ships had all the advantages. The real civilian ships were smart and pulled away from the weaponized ones. They watched as a pair of pleasure cruisers forced a weaponized cargo ship into the line of fire from one of the luxury liners.

"It worked?" Tristan breathed.

Emalynn shook her head. The royal and planetary forces quickly showed a strategy against the civilian-looking enemies that negated the advantage of greater numbers. Then the real scale of what they had done started to show. A message board sprang up with students from all over discussing strategies for finding the real ship among those listed. They were hacking into the minor systems on those ships, such as environmental controls.

"I think it's working." Emalynn pointed out the luxury liner they first noticed. One of its thrusters was firing randomly, making every shot it took miss.

#

TRISTAN – PRIME ORBIT

Watching the cleanup after the battle got boring almost as soon as it started. Tristan eagerly watched all the com lines for the next message from his father—for permission to land the shuttle. When it didn't come, he started scanning all the news sites and channels for anything about the coup attempt. There was plenty to see, including plenty of vids of Lord Leblanc being taken into custody. No one said anything at all about the twins or the Others' ship that was still in high orbit around Prime. Father must have been truly offended by Emalynn's behavior. Finally, he gave in to Emalynn's suggestion to swap favorite vids.

Three days after the battle, Tristan began to wonder if they'd been forgotten. The gossip sites had moved on to the upcoming cheerleading finals—which Emalynn insisted on watching. Tristan spent his time looking for anything interesting at all. He was almost bored enough to seek out exam prep sites.

"We are pleased to welcome Genise Stolvolker, spokeswoman for the royal family. Genise, it is good to see you."

Tristan pulled that site up to the full screen.

"Emalynn, you've got to see this."

Emalynn was stretching in the back. "Really?" She looked up. "Who's that?"

"Father's spokeswoman. She never goes on the gossip shows."

Emalynn let out a sigh but came up to see what was happening. "This had better be someone telling us we can land."

Tristan nodded. "I did mention that code 58 comes with consequences. At least we aren't in a dungeon."

Emalynn growled.

"I've brought an announcement from His Royal Majesty, King Levon."

"How exciting. It's not often that you come to us for an official announcement."

Emalynn sat down. "What site is this?"

"Hot Topics."

"You're kidding me. They get an official announcement? The universe has gone crazy."

"So you're telling me that His Royal Majesty has some gossip he wants to tell the rest of us. You heard it here first—the king is human." The host said the joke with a nervous smile.

Genise gave a polite smile. "Of course. Their Royal Majesties care for all our people, and if you weren't so good at getting the dish out faster than they could, they'd be here more often."

The host's tight smile revealed she understood the veiled insult. Tristan caught Emalynn's look of amusement.

"So there *is* something we don't know yet?"

Genise nodded.

"Any hint?"

"Well, let's just say you've already picked up part of this story. We're just here to give the royal take on the subject. I'm sure your viewers will be thrilled."

Emalynn snorted. "Is she always this gossipy?"

Tristan shook his head. "She's good at being what people expect in the situation she's in. But mostly, she's on the news channels."

"So boring?"

"Yeah."

"Nice to know she can be a tease too."

Genise handed over a small disk. "I think we're ready to let you all in on the secret."

"Official secrets, should I be looking for the black ops?"

"This one has been tested and is safe." They both laughed.

The scene shifted to an image of King Levon and Queen Treylyn in the throne room. They were both in celebration costumes—the queen's a simple blue dress with silver trim, Father in a matching blue shirt and ankle-length black pants with silver threads woven in to make them sparkle. He had a darker blue jacket open to the waist with the royal crest on the lapel, and the crest of the royal house hung just in the middle of his chest.

"I want to thank everyone who participated in our recent contest seeking Prince Tristan." He bowed his head slightly. "There were millions of images to sort through, and it was a difficult decision. I'm pleased to announce that Davy Carlise-"

"Isn't that Murphy's friend?" Tristan asked.

Emalynn nodded.

"-and Karen Toya-"

"What about Dom?" Emalynn said. "She's going to be pissed."

"-have the best eye for Tristan and his lookalikes. They will be afforded an all-expenses paid trip to Prime to meet with Prince Tristan and his twin sister, Princess Emalynn."

Tristan stared at the screen.

"That's it?" Emalynn said. "They couldn't welcome us home before making a public announcement?"

"Remember how I said you were rude?"

"This is going to be… interesting."

<<<<>>>>